COYO

Buffalo hunter _____ is settling
down to a more civilized life in Fort
Revenge, in Indian Territory, helping
his friend run a stage line there.
However, it isn't long before trouble
comes from two directions: in the form
of an outlaw gang from Tulsa who
want to buy his friend's stagecoach
company and won't take no for an
answer, and from a family of killers
who are seeking revenge for the death
of their kin at his hands. O'Brien
must respond to these challenges with
his own brand of gunsmoke . . .

RALPH HAYES

COYOTE MOON

Complete and Unabridged

LINFORD
Leicester

First published in Great Britain in 2015 by
Robert Hale Limited
London

First Linford Edition
published 2018
by arrangement with
Robert Hale
an imprint of
The Crowood Press
Wiltshire

A catalogue record for this book is available
from the British Library.

ISBN 978–1–4448–3692–9

Published by
F. A. Thorpe (Publishing)
Anstey, Leicestershire

Set by Words & Graphics Ltd.
Anstey, Leicestershire
Printed and bound in Great Britain by
T. J. International Ltd., Padstow, Cornwall

This book is printed on acid-free paper

To my wife,
whose urgings and suggestions
inspired this story

1

Ezra Logan was the surviving patriarch of a dwindling family of horse-thieves and murderers.

Years ago he and his brother had organized a ruthless gang of cut-throats and hooligans which terrorized the whole territory of Montana for over a decade, until finally arousing so much revulsion from the law and citizenry that they had had to retreat to a small, back-country town in Colorado called Birney Pass.

Now at sixty-two and his brother gone, and recently his only son Gus, Ezra had just about given up the way of the gun and now depended on his kin to maintain the shrinking family coffers. On this balmy late-spring night, he sat drinking rum in his sprawling but primitive cabin, reminiscing about his violent past.

'You should have been at Missoula.

Taking the cash from that little outhouse of a bank there was like stealing turkeys from a wire pen. But then them yellow scum come with their shotguns and rifles, and the lead flew like you was in a hornet's nest. You should have been there.'

He was sitting at an oak table with his two grandsons Matt and Will, who lived with him and his wife Nettie, who was washing up dinner dishes nearby a crackling fireplace.

'I was only eight then,' young Will spoke up in a thin, reedy voice. He was a decade older now, sallow-faced, skinny and retarded.

'Shut up, Will,' his older brother Matt responded in a hard voice. He was five years senior to Will, with a lean, handsome face and dark hair. He wore an Iver-Johnson .32 revolver on a low-slung gunbelt. He was Ezra's protégé now that the boys' father Gus had been killed by a buffalo hunter a few weeks ago in a mountain cabin.

'Pa used to tell us about the Missoula

2

job,' Matt said. 'You come away from that with lead in your ribcage.'

'Lead in your ribcage!' Will echoed with a high giggle.

Ezra cast a slow, sober look on him. He was a brawny, gray-haired man with cold eyes and a scar running down his left cheek. 'I eat lead for breakfast,' he grated out. 'And I got four of them yellow-bellies myself that day. Blew the top plum off the head of one. You could look right inside it.' He grinned, remembering.

'Too bad you wasn't with Pa at that hunter's cabin,' Matt suggested. 'He might be alive now.'

'You talking about that devil from Hell that killed my Gus?' Nettie yelled in a high, cracking voice from across the room at the sink. 'I'd like to see that pond scum in Hell with his back broke!'

'Tend to your work, Nettie,' Ezra said evenly. He ruled what was left of his family with an iron fist. On his straight chair at his back hung his gunbelt holding a Tranter .38 revolver with carved notches on its bone grip. He looked over at Matt again. 'If I'd been at that cabin with your daddy, that hunter would've died a slow death.'

'Folks say Pa and that boy with him was stealing the hunter's pelts, and he caught them,' Will's high, thin voice interrupted them. He always had a vacant, dull look in his rheumy eyes, and a nervous habit of nodding his head repetitively when others were talking. When Ezra's son Gus had announced the boy's condition when Will was very young, Ezra had seriously suggested Gus take the child out behind a shed and 'put him out of his misery'. Now, at the table he gave Will another dark look.

'That hunter went south,' Ezra went on. 'We heard he would be headed to Indian Territory, through Kansas. He's supposedly got a friend down there in a place called Fort Revenge. That would take him pretty well past a stink-hole in Kansas named Sulphur Creek, where your uncle Hank owns a saloon. But I

4

told you all this. I wired Hank to watch for the hunter and kill him if he come upon him.'

'His name is O'Brien,' Will piped up.

'We know the hunter's name,' Matt growled at his brother. 'Go get some coffee from your grandma.'

'I ain't thirsty.'

'I'm about ready to send another telegram,' Ezra said. 'I should have heard back from Hank by now.'

'I heard stuff about him,' Will intervened again, dull eyes wide.

They both cast brittle looks on him.

'In Laramie he walked through a hail of lead to kill a man with his bare fists.'

'Where did you hear that bull pucky?' Matt grated out.

'When we was over at Fort Griffin. Some traders there. They say he don't carry a sidearm but gunfighters avoid him. He talks five Indian tongues, and the Lakota say he can't be killed with a bullet.' He stammered over his words. Had a big grin.

'For God's sake!' Matt muttered,

shaking his head.

Ezra reached over and slapped Will violently across the face, knocking him off his chair. He hit the floor with a thump, holding his cheek.

'Hey!' Tears welled in his eyes.

'No more about that no-good, murdering hunter!' Ezra spat out.

Nettie came hurrying over and helped Will to his feet. 'Come on, boy. You don't belong with the men. I'll get you a corn muffin.' A scowl at Ezra. 'I told you to lay off this poor thing. He's like a crippled bird.'

'I shoot crippled birds,' Ezra answered. 'Just keep him away from me. Gus should have used a bat on him when he was three.'

Will moved off with Nettie, and Matt glanced over at his grandfather. 'Hank might have already done it for us. Send a second wire tomorrow.'

He had just finished speaking when a knocking came at the cabin door. It was night outside so the two men eyed each other suspiciously. Ezra retrieved his

Tranter from the chair and went to the door. 'Who is it?' he called out.

A muffled response. 'It's Murdoch. From the saloon in town.'

Ezra knew the man. He opened the door, his gun still in hand. 'Yeah, Murdoch? What is it? You been drinking?'

'Well, yeah.' The skinny fellow grinned slightly. But his face immediately went sober again. 'You got a wire. From Sulphur Creek in Kansas. A guy named Jennings. Worked for your nephew Hank, I guess.' He handed Ezra a paper.

'I kind of read it, Ezra.'

Ezra didn't look at the paper. 'Well? What did it say?'

Murdoch took a deep breath in. 'Hank's dead, Ezra.'

Ezra's thick face went taut. 'What?'

Matt got up and walked over there. 'Did you say dead?'

'He got into it with a fellow named O'Brien and O'Brien killed him.'

Ezra's face went pale.

'Sonofabitch,' Matt muttered.

'Sorry, Ezra,' Murdoch said quietly.

Then he was gone.

Ezra closed the door and went back to the table in a daze, and sat down heavily. He read the wire. Matt came and read it, too. 'Sonofabitch,' he said.

Nettie came up to them, a small, stooped woman with knotted gray hair. Will was just behind her. 'Did I hear right? That hunter killed Hank?'

'That's right,' Matt said heavily.

She let out a moan. 'That devil from Hell's got to be killed, Ezra! Him and his kin and all his friends, and their bodies burned on a pyre of flame!'

'Shut up, Nettie,' Ezra said in a low voice.

'Nobody ever beat the hunter in a fight,' Will blurted out, then stepped back two steps.

Ezra hurled a blistering look at him, but spoke to Matt. 'Well, with Hank gone, I guess it's up to us, Matt.'

Matt's face was clouded with anger. 'If that bastard don't go to Hell, no Logan can ever show his face in public again.'

Ezra met his angry look. 'Are you as good with that gun as everybody says you are, boy?'

Matt nodded. 'I'm the best in this whole damn state, Ezra.'

'Good. Get ready to ride. You and me are heading out tomorrow to put this rotten scum in his grave. Then it will be over.'

'Where are we going?'

'We'll head for Sulphur Creek, confirm that he rode on south to join some friend of his in Fort Revenge. Then we'll run him down there and kill him.'

Matt slapped his hand on the table. 'And that hound will pay for murdering my daddy.'

'And your uncle Hank,' Ezra added. 'Now let's get some packing done.'

★ ★ ★

The following morning, in rocky, butte-and-sagebrush country a day's ride west of Fort Revenge, O'Brien knelt at the side of a shallow stream examining a trap he had set for beavers. The trap was empty, and he placed it back in the gurgling water, upstream fifty yards from a beaver dam. He stopped and straightened up for a moment, thinking he had heard something in the small woods behind him. He turned, scanned the trees with piercing blue eyes, and then returned to make sure the trap was positioned as he wanted it.

He was a big man, but trim and athletic-looking, wearing rawhides, stovepipe boots and a trail-dusty Stetson. He had a trimmed, full beard, and his long hair under the Stetson was showing some gray in it. A buffalo hunter put out of business by the big hide companies, he had gone to trapping for a living and had come to Fort Revenge because his friend there had written to him saying the trapping was still good in this area, and O'Brien had stayed on to ply his new trade and help his friend Smith run his stagecoach line.

The trap positioned properly now, he rose and shook the water from his big hands. A faint scent came to his nostrils, and then the sound again. He turned quickly to the treeline, under thirty yards distant, and saw the big cat for the first time.

It was the biggest cougar he had ever seen. It stood just outside the trees on flat, damp ground that separated it from O'Brien.

'Sonofabitch,' O'Brien muttered.

He should have paid more attention when he heard the first sound. Mistakes like that could cost a man his life out here. His Appaloosa was picketed a hundred yards down-stream with O'Brien's rifles on its irons, and he never carried a sidearm. His friend Shanghai Smith was a mile away, checking his own traps.

O'Brien felt like a fool. He swore again at himself. The cougar, a hulking, muscular animal, was staring right into his eyes. It moved forward a few paces, and stopped.

O'Brien had been threatened by grizzlies, wolves, and stampeding buffalo, but had never been stalked seriously by a cougar. And the look in this cat's eyes revealed that it was very serious about O'Brien, and was readying itself for a deadly attack.

It advanced another few yards, and growled menacingly. O'Brien glanced down the creek toward his horse, which was barely visible around a bend in the stream. O'Brien heard it whinny nervously, and scowled.

'Now you warn me, damn you,' he said quietly, in his throat.

The cougar was just ten yards away, and now it circled to his left. Carefully. Calculatedly. It wanted to get in a good position. Big cats preferred to attack from the rear or side, to get at the neck of the prey and crush it. O'Brien turned with the cougar, keeping them face to face.

He reached for the skinning knife he usually kept in his boot sheath, but then remembered he had lent the knife to Smitty earlier, because his friend had left his own at their hardship camp.

O'Brien yelled at the animal, waving

his arms. It crouched, but did not retreat. It circled back the other way, coming clear around to his other side, trying to find a way in that satisfied it. Yellow eyes burning, growling sounds coming from its throat, it feinted a charge at him, and dropped back.

O'Brien knew that if the cat found a vulnerable stance to attack, he was as good as dead. It had a lot more weapons than he did. The cougar started back around him again in a narrower circle. For the first time, O'Brien spotted a short length of driftwood lying a few feet away, near the water. He edged over to it, keeping his face to the cougar. A moment later he had it in his hand.

It was a pitiful weapon. Less than three feet of tree branch, with a couple of offshoots jutting out an inch or two. He got a good grip on it and waved it at the cat.

It was not impressed.

It started in on him, but he swung the stick and it backed off slightly. The cougar wanted to circle him swiftly and come in from behind, but the stream was behind O'Brien, and he wasn't about to leave that cover.

Finally the cougar made the half-circle a last time, and got a partial view of O'Brien's neck from the side, and suddenly sprang at him, eyes fiery coals, inch-long fangs bared wide.

Halfway through its leap, O'Brien swung the club and struck the animal violently in its face, as it was in mid-air. The club slammed hard into the cougar's mouth and eyes and one of the jutting barbs slashed into the cat's right eye. The weight of the animal brought it on to him, and he felt the heavy body crash into his chest and arms, and he went down, hitting the wet sand with a thud.

But the cougar jumped off him wildly, shaking its head with a sticky wetness running down from its destroyed right eye. Yowling and twisting its body. As O'Brien watched, the big cat turned and raced off into the trees, disappearing there.

O'Brien fell back on to the sand, just

lying quietly for a moment, the stream gurgling at his back. The sounds of the cougar gone now. He threw the club into the water and it drifted away from him.

'Mangy damn cat!' he grumbled, lying there. He rose slowly to his feet, and looked himself over. There was a rip in the rawhide tunic, and a shallow gash on his chest beneath it. There was also a scratch on his cheek that would heal quickly.

'Damn lucky,' he admitted aloud. 'And damn stupid.'

Just at that moment, Shanghai Smith came riding along the beach toward him. 'Hallo there! Your horse is going crazy! Any trouble?'

As Smith reined in a few feet away, O'Brien gave him a weary look. 'Just been petting a pussy cat out of the woods. I sent him off to set on somebody else's lap.'

'My God, look at you.'

'Let's get back to camp,' O'Brien grunted. 'I'm so hungry I could eat my boots, nails and all.'

A few moments later, they were heading back down the strip of sand.

⋆   ⋆   ⋆

Later that day, back at Fort Revenge, a small knot of men rode into town.

There were four of them. They were all dressed in dark clothing and rode dark-brown geldings. Led by Frank Provost, he and his men had ridden all the way from Tulsa because they had heard that Fort Revenge was a prosperous little town with good business opportunities. There was a general store, a boarding-house, the Prairie Café and, most important, the Territorial Express Stagecoach Company. It was the stage company that interested Provost most, but he had decided that if he liked the town, he would prefer owning everything. The Territorial Express was owned by Shanghai Smith, with O'Brien a minor partner. They split their time between the business and trapping.

16

'Hey, my information was right,' Provost said to the man sitting his mount beside him. 'This town looks sweet. I think I could like this.' He was a dark, lean man, rather handsome, wearing a long riding coat and a dark-blue vest. He had stashed away quite a pile of cash robbing banks and stages in Kansas and Missouri, and now wanted to go legitimate. In amassing his savings, he had had to kill five men, but had no remorse about it.

The man sitting beside him was his right-hand man, Ira Skinner. He gazed across the dirt street to the Prairie Café. 'Not bad. And there ain't no law here, Frank. It's kind of tailor-made for us.' He was a brawny, tough-looking man with straw-like hair and a broken nose. He was fast with a gun, but not as fast as Provost.

'I'm hungry!' came the thin voice of one of the men riding behind them. It was Icepick Munro, who had black coals for eyes in a pale, sallow face. A tic pulled at his mouth at the end of his speech. He was a deranged killer who preferred knives to guns, and in his early days had killed at least two men with an icepick.

'You're always hungry,' the fellow beside him said caustically. 'But the only thing you ever eat is raw steak. It's disgusting.' The fourth man was Slim Latham, the newest of the gang. He had a wandering left eye and a bony face. He enjoyed using his gun, and was an unpredictable subordinate. But so far Provost hadn't had any real trouble from him.

'Let's go get us something to eat at that pretty little restaurant over there,' Provost said, grinning. 'Introduce ourselves. Maybe do some business.'

'I don't care about no business,' the fellow called Icepick grumbled. 'My insides has been gnawing at me all afternoon.'

Nobody paid any attention to him. Provost spurred his gelding across the street, and the others followed. In front of the Prairie Café they dismounted, looking tough and dangerous. They

18

swaddled reins over a hitching post, and climbed steps up to the entrance, looking around.

Inside, several customers were already seated at tables having an early evening meal. Locals, enjoying a brief social hour. At the table nearest the door sat three drivers of the Territorial Express, and at another, across the room, were two women seated with the Mayor of Fort Revenge, one Avery Spencer. The two women were boarders at a local rooming-house, and both employees of the village under Spencer. Abigail Pritchard was middle-aged and a kind of town clerk, and the other was Spencer's book-keeper, a much younger, rather pretty woman who was new to Fort Revenge and the West. Her name was Sarah Carter, and she had come to Indian Territory as a mail-order bride, but it hadn't worked out.

'Say, Mr Mayor!' yelled one of the drivers. 'When are you going to fix that pothole in front of the Express? I almost broke a wheel yesterday!' It was R.C. Funk, the senior driver at the table. He was short, with a protruding belly, and wore a wrinkled vest over a checkered shirt.

'We talk business at the office!' Abigail called back.

Ben Thatcher, the new owner of the café, came out of the kitchen carrying a coffee pot. He walked over to the mayor's table. 'Another cup, Mr Mayor? Ladies?'

They all refused, and he headed for the other table. Just as he got there, the door swung open and the four riders from the street filed in. Their spurs made metallic whisperings on the hand-rived wooden floor.

'Afternoon, gentlemen,' Thatcher greeted them with a nervous grin, looking them over slowly. 'Find yourself a table and I'll be right with you.'

None of them made any response. Provost had discarded his riding coat and now appeared in a dark shirt under the blue vest. On his hip hung a wicked-looking Colt Army .45, slung low and menacing. The four of them took a table on a side wall, away from the other two.

'You sell drinks in here?' the blocky Skinner growled out.

Thatcher touched the coffee pot absently with his free hand, and burned it. He sucked his breath in and shook the hand. 'We got beer and ale, boys.'

'Bring us a pitcher of beer,' Provost told him. 'And four steaks.'

'Don't fry mine,' sallow-faced Icepick called out. The tic jerked at his mouth. 'Just a trace of brown on both sides.' A Starr .44 stuck out ominously from his hip below table level.

'You got it, boys,' Thatcher replied, and disappeared into the kitchen.

All eyes focused on the newcomers as soon as they had entered the place. Sarah Carter had seen men before who looked like this, and her face had gone sober. Her new friend O'Brien, who had found her alone on the prairie and had brought her here, had had to save her from a man like these whom she had intended to marry.

A second stage driver, Ed Reece,

turned to the four. 'I reckon you boys is new in town.'

The four just stared at him. After a moment, Provost replied, 'Just rode in. You got a pretty little town here.'

'Pretty little town,' Icepick echoed him.

Slim Latham, who lusted for all young women, and had a history of rape in three states, was already eyeing pretty Sarah.

The third driver, nicknamed Old Scratch, a gray-haired, hard-bitten older man, now spoke up. 'There ain't a nicer town in the whole damn territory!'

Icepick shook his head. 'What do you do around here, Grandpa? Sweep up horse manure from the street?'

Old Scratch's face showed quick anger, but Funk laid a hand on his arm.

Now Mayor Spencer turned to them. 'You boys just passing through? Mrs Barstow might put you up in her boarding-house.'

'Actually,' Provost responded, 'I been

thinking about buying the place.'

A heavy silence crowded into the room. Sarah and her friend turned to stare at the newcomers. Sarah had noticed the guns, and the manner of their owners, and figured they could mean trouble. The mayor tried an uncertain smile.

'I don't understand,' he said. 'You want to buy what?'

'I mean, your town,' Provost said easily. He let a slow grin take over his aquiline face.

R.C. Funk frowned. 'What the hell are you saying, mister?'

'Take it easy, R.C.,' Spencer said quietly. He addressed Provost again. 'My name is Spencer, I'm the mayor here. If you're thinking of investing, I can't think of any business that's up for sale.'

'Well, we'll see,' Provost countered. 'I haven't made my offers yet.' He rested a hand on the Colt revolver at his hip, holding Spencer's gaze with a mild one.

Thatcher came out with the pitcher

of beer, and poured it for them. 'Them steaks will be right out, boys.'

'How about you, fry cook?' Provost said to him. 'How much would you take for this grease pot?'

Thatcher regarded him curiously. 'To sell it? Why, I just bought it. I expect to make a nice living here.'

Icepick had just retrieved a Tulsa newspaper from an adjacent table, and was studying the front page. 'Well, what do you think of this! They built one of them stage theaters in London, and they say it's got real electric lights. By Jesus, do you give that credence?'

Skinner gave him a fierce look, and Thatcher took that opportunity to retreat to the kitchen. Icepick shrugged and threw the paper on the floor.

'Maybe I'll buy the general store first,' Provost went on, as if Icepick hadn't spoken. 'Of course, my main interest is in the stage line.'

Ed Reece leaned forward. 'The Express is owned by Shanghai Smith, mister, and his friend O'Brien. I know Smith wouldn't sell. He ain't interested.'

'That's right!' Funk said loudly.

'Are you boys drivers?' Provost asked calmly.

'That's right.' From Reece. 'And because of us the Express is a going success!'

Sarah turned to Provost again. 'You men are misguided in your plans. You'd better look elsewhere for investment.'

Latham's eyes narrowed down on her, and he felt a hunger awakening in him. 'Looks like we got us a real honey badger here, boys.'

'Well, well,' Skinner grinned. 'The chorus line is heard from.'

'Do you know Smith too?' Provost said to her pleasantly.

'I do, and I know his partner. I wouldn't recommend you make any trouble for him.'

Latham got up slowly, and walked over to her table. 'You smell good, honey. I can smell you way over there.' He reached down and touched her dark hair. Sarah flinched away, gasping slightly.

The mayor frowned. 'Leave the

women alone now, boys. We don't want any trouble in here.'

'You mean to give us trouble, mister?' Latham said in a threatening tone.

'Latham,' Provost called out. 'Come on back over here.'

Latham gave him a scathing look. 'I'm just talking here.'

Provost hesitated. 'Your steak will be here any minute.'

Latham focused his wandering left eye that had struck fear into women and girls on previous occasions. 'Yeah. Steak.' He leaned over Sarah. 'You and me will talk some other time, sweetheart. Where it's more private.'

Latham returned to his table, and Provost addressed the mayor. 'Is either of these owners available to talk with today?'

'They're both out trapping,' R.C. Funk intervened. 'Might be weeks before they get back here. I wouldn't wait.'

Skinner glowered at him. 'Boy, you're brash as a flour peddler running for governor.'

Icepick glanced at the discarded newspaper. 'I just don't give that credence. That London thing.'

'Icepick,' Provost said in a quiet voice.

'Yeah?'

'You mention that paper again, I'll blow your liver out through your back.' He hadn't even looked toward Icepick through the admonition.

All eyes at the other tables turned on Provost soberly.

'I'm just saying,' Icepick mumbled almost inaudibly.

Seeing the attention he had created, Provost allowed a smile to play across his mouth. 'Don't pay any attention, folks. We just josh with one another. You understand.'

Spencer shook his head. 'I don't think we got your name, Mr — '

'Provost,' was the measured response.

Ed Reece's eyes narrowed. 'Frank Provost? The man that's wanted for bank and stage robbery in three states?'

Provost's eyes and tone went flat for

the first time. 'I'm not wanted here in the Territory. And those charges against me are false.'

Sarah and Spencer exchanged a look. Spencer rose, and the women followed. 'Mr Provost, no offense, but I recommend you and your men move on when your mounts are rested up. There's nothing in Fort Revenge for you.'

Provost grinned. 'Oh, we're just moseying around this trip. Testing the waters, so to speak. We'll be riding back to Tulsa this evening. I have other business there. But we'll be back, Mr Mayor. And then we'll have some further talk with some of your more prominent citizens. I'm looking forward to it.'

'Where the hell are them steaks?' Latham called out to the kitchen.

A moment later the mayor, the women, and the drivers were all gone.

The Provost gang ate their meals leisurely, and while the sun was still an hour from setting over nearby low buttes they were riding back out of town. As they rode past the Territorial Express building, R.C. Funk was sitting outside and watched as the four riders went past, guns bristling noticeably on their hips.

None of them glanced at him except Icepick, who threw a tough grin at Funk. Then they were out of sight around a bend.

Funk breathed out a relieved sigh, and wished for the swift return of Smith and O'Brien.

They might be needed sooner than either of them knew.

2

A couple of hours after the Provost gang had ridden out of Fort Revenge, Shanghai Smith and O'Brien made hardship camp on the bank of the same stream they had been trapping in earlier. They had a small camp-fire going, and they had a rabbit roasting over it that O'Brien had shot not long after his encounter with the cougar. They were seated around the fire on folding camp-stools brought with them from town and Smith was fishing in a burlap bag for corn dodgers. O'Brien held a steaming tin cup of coffee in his trail-coarsened hand.

'This is right civilized next to the old days,' Smith said in a booming voice. Other buffalo hunters said he could be heard over a herd of stampeding buffalo while speaking in a normal voice. 'Remember, partner? Stuffing down dry soda biscuits from a flour sack and boiling chicory coffee in a tin can. Salt pork fried on a green stick. We saved the fry grease for oiling our boots and saddles.'

O'Brien nodded. 'Remember it? Hell, I was still doing it till I rode into Fort Revenge a little while ago.'

The grin eased off Smith's face. 'Oh. Sure. He studied his friend's pensive, ruggedly handsome face. O'Brien had discarded his Stetson and his long hair was wild around his face. 'Are you missing that already?' Smith concluded.

'I ain't had a chance to settle in at the depot yet,' O'Brien told him. 'I'll be all right.' He turned the spit the rabbit hung on, and the fire crackled.

Smith laid the corn muffins on a piece of groundcloth, and rested his thick hands on his knees. He was an enormous man. O'Brien was big, but Smith was an inch taller and weighed fifty pounds more than O'Brien, with a hefty belly. He had been one of the best, and had partnered O'Brien several times. O'Brien had always admired his toughness and his fearlessness in the face of danger.

'Before we got into it,' Smith went on in his loud voice, 'them fancy boys from Europe come and shot the shaggies just for sport.' His voice lowered, and he looked into the fire.

He was referring to the organized hunting parties that were popular when the buffalo were thick on the plains. A feather would be tossed to test the wind direction, and then men stripped to the waist, kerchiefs around their heads, and would spur their mounts into the thick herds, rifle in one hand and a ramrod in the other, mouths jammed with cartridges, firing wildly into the herd, bringing down all the animals they could before the herd disappeared into the distance.

'They didn't hurt the big herds,' O'Brien said. 'It was the commercial hide companies. Come in and clean out a whole herd in an hour. Skin hides off and leave the meat to spoil in the sun.'

'General Phil Sheridan said to let the big companies hunt at will, because the disappearance of the herds made the Indians easier to control,' Smith remembered. 'Well. Maybe he was right.'

O'Brien gave him a sober look. 'One Lakota warrior is worth ten Sheridan,' he said, in a low, hard voice.

Smith met his serious look. 'Well, yeah. I see what you mean. Of course, it was Jackson who moved them all into the Territory here.'

'A man ought to be able to live where he wants,' O'Brien said. 'Whether he's rancher or Indian.'

Smith nodded, and got up and examined the rabbit 'It's about done. Say, you ought to put some of that axle grease on your cat scratches. That can infect.'

'All right, nursie,' O'Brien said with a grin, a rarity for him. Smith was a stalwart riding partner, but he had always talked too much. 'You're as bad as Sarah when I got shot.'

Smith grinned. 'I wish I had that

pretty a gal sweet on me.'

O'Brien frowned at him. 'She ain't sweet on me,' he growled. 'She's grateful because I saved her from that would-be groom Jake Latimer. That's all it is, Smitty. Don't make it more than that.'

Smith raised his big hands defensively. 'Hey. Maybe I'm wrong, partner. Don't pay no attention to me. But you did save her butt before that when you found her all alone out on the prairie with her drivers dead, with redskin arrows sticking out of them. Why wouldn't she think you're special?'

O'Brien gave him a silent reprimand with a stony look. The fire crackled and sparks flew up into the blackness of the night. He took the rabbit off the spit and carved it up with his Bowie skinning knife, and they sat back and chewed on the meat and corn dodgers. After a while Smith spoke again with his mouth full.

'You said you had some trouble in Sulphur Creek before you found Sarah out there.'

O'Brien sighed. 'Ain't that rabbit enough to keep your mouth busy, partner?'

Smith raised thick eyebrows. 'I was just wondering.'

'Sulphur Creek was took over by gunfighters, and we had to clean them out. One of them was a yellow bastard called Logan. I had come on his kin in Colorado when him and a second weasel tried to steal my pelts. I had to kill them, and then his people up there demanded that Hank Logan avenge that first boy's death. But I killed him, too, cleaning up the town because a boy I knew there was in danger.'

'Won't the kinfolk up in Colorado get a little ruffled by that second killing?'

O'Brien took a swig of hot coffee. 'Smitty, if I worried over stuff like that, I'd be dead of brain fatigue long ago.'

Smith shook his head. 'Sometimes I think trouble just sticks to you like the cholera to an Indian.'

'I never run from it,' O'Brien admitted. 'It don't seem worth it.' He set a tin plate down beside the fire. 'Smitty, now that I've invested in the stage line, just what work do you have planned for me when we get back to town?'

Smith put his plate down too. He blew his heavy cheeks out. 'Well, I got so much paperwork to do. I thought you could arrange driver schedules. Talk to some bankers about carrying their shipments with us. Ride shotgun when you get the urge. Oversee the drivers when they're at the depot. Stuff like that.' He watched O'Brien's face. 'Does that sound OK to you?'

O'Brien stared into the fire. 'I'll do anything I can to help out,' he said quietly. 'I just hope . . . '

'Hope what?'

'I hope I'm cut out for this, Smitty. I don't want to let you down. All I've known all my life is the trail. The call of the wild.'

Smith studied his friend's rugged face. 'I felt the same way when I come here to go into business, partner. I'd lie awake nights wishing I was back out there, breaking every rise on my belly like a goddamn snake, keeping out of sight of the herd till it was time to go in. I dreamt about it and you was often part of them dreams.'

O'Brien glanced over at him, and sipped the coffee again. 'We ain't took many skins so far this time, Smitty.'

Smith sighed. 'I know. When I wrote you, the Kiowa was reporting heavy takes of beaver hereabouts. Even some ermine and fox. Things have tapered off, I reckon. Sorry I give you a wrong steer. But I'm sure glad you're here. I needed somebody like you. None of my drivers has got the sense he was born with. Nobody that can take charge. You and me can make the Express one of the best companies in the Territory.'

O'Brien nodded soberly. 'I just thought there would be more of this. But I'll make the best of it, Smitty. The West we knew is about gone, anyway. I reckon we have to change with the times.'

'Hell, there's even a brand-new federation of labor unions back East now,' Smith said, shaking his head. 'If that creeps out here, my drivers will demand a living wage and put us out of business!' He let out his booming laugh.

O'Brien held a hand up for silence. He had heard a sound in the darkness, a rider heading toward them. He reached for his Winchester lever-action repeating rifle that lay on a blanket near him. They both stared toward the sound of hoofbeats, and in a moment a rider appeared in the firelight.

The rider stopped at the edge of their camp, and tipped a dusty hat. 'Evening, boys. Can you spare a weary traveler a cup of your coffee?' He was obviously not a ranch hand. He wore a dark suit coat, red vest, and fancy boots. He was apparently not carrying iron. O'Brien kept the Winchester in his right hand.

It was trail courtesy to be hospitable to another traveler. Smith nodded to O'Brien, then spoke to the stranger.

'Come on in, stranger. We can spare you a cup.' He was wearing his Joslyn .44 at his thick waist and a Henry rifle lay nearby on a ground blanket. But this fellow didn't seem to be any trouble.

Their visitor dismounted and picketed his mount with a picket stake, then came over by the fire and O'Brien handed him a cup of hot coffee.

'I'm Jeff Akers from Tulsa,' he announced.

'You a gambler?' Smith asked.

Akers grinned thinly. He was tall, slim, and svelte-looking. 'I guess it shows.'

'Live and let live,' Smith said. 'I'm Shanghai Smith, and that ornery bastard over there is O'Brien.'

Akers nodded, staring at O'Brien. 'I think I know that name.'

O'Brien just sat there. He laid the rifle down beside him.

'Are you the buffalo hunter from up north?' Akers pursued.

'I done some hunting,' O'Brien

replied, not looking at him. He sipped his own coffee, looking into the fire. He wouldn't have invited the stranger in.

Akers snapped his fingers. 'That's it! You're the one they call the White Lakota!'

O'Brien turned a brittle look on him but remained silent.

'O'Brien don't talk much about his past,' Smith offered, watching O'Brien's face.

But Akers wasn't paying attention. 'Yes, I remember now. You're the hunter who made John Ringo back down! Up in Wichita or Dodge. Am I right?'

O'Brien rose slowly, and when Akers saw his face, he took a step backwards without knowing he had done it.

'Does coffee always make your mouth run like this, boy? You better finish that cup and be on your way.'

Akers swallowed hard. 'Sorry. Me and my big mouth.' He swigged his coffee and coughed slightly.

Smith smiled a fat smile. 'You take your time, Akers. My partner had a bad day of trapping.' O'Brien walked over to his tethered Appaloosa just a short distance away, paying no further attention to them. 'Anything going on in Tulsa?' Smith added.

Akers watched O'Brien warily. 'Uh. Nothing worth reporting. Got taken in a card game by a fellow called Provost. Kept talking about taking over some town. He was heading out that very day.'

'Taking a town?' Smith said, with a frown.

'Yeah. Some place called Fort Revenge. I think that was it.'

O'Brien, over at his mount, turned toward Akers with narrowed eyes.

'Did you say Fort Revenge?' Smith said in a low voice.

'Why, yes. I'm pretty sure. I guess there's a stage company there. He kept on about running it himself.'

Smith grimaced. 'What the hell!'

Akers laid his empty cup on the ground, and wiped at his mouth. 'Well. I guess I'll be on my way.' He shot another scared look at O'Brien. 'Appreciate your hospitality, boys.' He started for his mount.

'Just a minute, mister,' came O'Brien's hard voice.

Akers turned as O'Brien walked over to him. In a moment they were nose to nose and Akers was suddenly breathless with the proximity of this primitive-looking man. 'Are you sure about all this?' O'Brien demanded.

Akers just wanted to get out of there now. 'I'm just telling you what I heard, O'Brien. What's the trouble?'

Smith was recovering from the news. 'I own the Territorial Express,' he said. 'We do.' Motioning toward O'Brien.

'Oh,' Akers said in a half-whisper.

'You think he's already there?' Smith said.

Akers shrugged. 'He could be. I got the idea he was just making a cursory visit this time.'

O'Brien had never heard the word 'cursory' before. 'Why don't you try to talk English?' he said in a frigid voice.

'I think he means he was just going to case the place for a future visit,' Smith spoke up in a somber tone. Then he got an angry look on his face. 'Who the hell is this Provost: a banker?'

'He didn't look like a banker,' Akers said. 'He looked more like a gunfighter.'

O'Brien and Smith exchanged a dark look.

'All right,' O'Brien told their visitor. 'Get on your mount and get out.'

Akers looked sheepish. 'Sorry I mentioned it,' he said.

A few moments later he was mounted and gone.

'Well,' Smith finally grunted.

'Looks like the trapping is over for this trip out,' O'Brien suggested.

'We'll leave at sunrise tomorrow,' Smith agreed.

★　★　★

At that same hour in the bustling town of Tulsa, a two-hours' ride south of Fort Revenge, Frank Provost sat at a rear table at the Staked Plain Saloon. He was with Ira Skinner, but Icepick Munro had opted to remain at their hotel down the street, keeping away from Provost until his boss started talking to him again. Slim Latham was across town at a whorehouse dickering with a madam over the price of a redheaded prostitute.

Not far from Provost's table where he and Skinner nursed a bottle of Planters' Rye, a piano player was pounding out a chorus of 'Rally Round the Flag, Boys' to a scattered audience more interested in their drinks than music. Out on the street, an occasional cowpoke would ride up and down firing off his six-shooter into the blackness and shouting invectives at passers-by.

'If that bastard plays another of them Yankee songs, I'm going to throw him out into the street and shoot up his piano,' Skinner grumbled to Provost.

A winner at a faro table nearby yelled out his excitement, and Skinner turned and glared in that direction.

'What the hell is the matter with you tonight?' Provost said, swigging a shot glass of whiskey. 'You're skittery as a hog on ice.'

Skinner looked over at him. 'You told Barnes to meet you here a half-hour ago. I told you he wouldn't come. We don't need this. You don't need the money.'

'When somebody owes me money, I collect,' Provost said. 'He wanted five hundred to bribe a marshal down in Pike's Crossroads. Said I'd get a thousand back. When I saw him yesterday, he said he'd have it tonight.'

'He's probably in New Orleans by now,' Skinner said, throwing down some more of the rye.

'I could use that money for Fort Revenge,' Provost said. 'I've only got a thousand in the bank. I'll draw that out tomorrow. It will be mostly for the express company.'

'I don't understand you. Why offer them anything? Why not just take it? Who's going to stop you?'

Provost shook his head. 'Now, see, Skinner. That's why I'm running this show and you never will.' Skinner gave him a narrow look, and Provost continued, 'I want anything we do there to be all legal-like, in case we get trouble from it later. I'm going to get bills of sale, deeds. I already have the papers. I'm not going to offer much, of course. Just enough to show money exchanged hands. Our guns will be behind our offers.'

Skinner thought about that. 'I have to admit you've give it a lot of thought, Frank. But why don't we get out of here and hit that saloon down the street? This music is giving me a goddamn headache.'

At that moment, Icepick pushed through the swinging doors at the front of the saloon. He spotted his two cohorts immediately and walked on back to them.

'I almost fell asleep back there at the hotel.' He had been drinking. He eyed the pianist darkly, and walked over and slammed the lid down on to the fellow's hands. The music stopped abruptly, the player yelling out in pain.

'Shut that noise up!' Icepick yelled at the man.

'What the hell!' the fellow cried out, rubbing his bruised hands.

'Hey, what's going on over there?' called a hefty bartender across the room.

'It's all right, barkeep,' Provost shouted. 'Just a little disagreement. Any damage, I'll pay for it.'

The injured pianoman gave Icepick a hard scowl and left for a back room.

'Get the hell over here, Icepick,' Provost said heavily.

Icepick came over and sat down. In addition to the Starr .44 on his hip, he also had a Bowie knife in a leather sheath on his other side. He enjoyed using the knife more than the gun. 'I told you, Frank, he don't know no good songs. Maybe that will keep him quiet for a while.'

Skinner chuckled softly, and Provost

gave him an icy look. 'How many times have I told you?' he said. 'You only cause trouble when I tell you to. That stuff can rub off on me.'

Icepick shrugged. 'That boy gets under my skin.'

A big man came over to their table from across the room. He was very inebriated, weaving around as he spoke. 'Hey. What did you do to my piano player?'

Icepick glanced at him. 'That little ferret is all right. He's lucky I didn't smash his goddamn piano.'

'Now I wouldn't take kindly to that,' the big fellow slurred out. He carried an old pistol on his side but had forgotten it was even there.

Icepick stood up slowly, and drew the Bowie from its sheath. 'You want to make something of it?' he said in a sibilant whisper.

The big man looked at the knife and his face changed. 'Well, if you put it that way. I reckon he can probably take care of hisself OK.' He turned quickly away and staggered back to his table. Icepick sat back down, the knife sheathed.

'Do you see what I mean?' Provost said irritably.

Icepick arched his brow. 'I didn't invite him over here. Sorry, Frank.'

'You should have stayed at the hotel,' Provost said. 'You're less trouble there.'

'Oh. I talked to somebody at the hotel. Turns out he knows this Shanghai Smith. He won't cause you no trouble.'

Provost frowned at him. 'Why is that?'

'That boy is an old buffalo hunter, gray-haired and fat. Wears a sidearm but probably don't know how to use it. Spent his whole life shooting long guns. The hotel guy didn't know anything about the other partner. He's new to Fort Revenge, and the word is he don't even carry a gun. This will be a pushover, believe me.'

Provost was about to reply to him when Skinner interrupted. 'I think that's your boy that just come in.'

Provost and Icepick turned and saw a tall, lean man standing just inside the doors. His right eye was a milky white which gave him a bizarre look. Two Colt revolvers hung on his hips like small cannons. He spotted Provost, and came over.

'Frank,' he greeted Provost. He had an easy, confident manner. He looked around the table at the other two, as they studied the milky eye.

'Barnes. Good to see you could get here.' He had given up on Barnes showing at all. 'These are the friends I told you about. Skinner and Munro. Take some weight off.'

Barnes assessed Provost's face as he seated himself. 'I thought you'd be alone, Frank.'

'Oh, these boys know all my business.' Provost smiled. 'Have a drink.'

Barnes poured himself a whiskey and swigged it down. He was a moderately skilled gunfighter who had worked briefly with Provost before Provost had formed this gang, when he was in

Missouri. He wiped a hand across his mouth.

'I got some cash for you, Frank.'

Provost grinned slightly. 'Well. Miracles do happen. I've been waiting for payment for some time, Barnes. Any extra for me? Like you said?'

Barnes got a worried look in his good eye, and poured himself another drink, and downed it. 'I don't have it all, Frank. I've had a run of bad luck. Lost some at that gambling hall down the street. They cheated me, the bastards.'

Provost looked down at his empty shot glass. His face had gone somber. 'Just how much do you have?'

Barnes sneaked a quick look at Provost. 'I've got two hundred.'

Icepick gave a quiet laugh, and Skinner shook his head. Provost just sat there looking at his empty glass for a long moment.

'I can get more tomorrow,' Barnes said hurriedly. 'There's this guy that owes me from way back. He's good for it, Frank. Five hundred at least. I'll meet you back here at the same time tomorrow night. I'm trying hard to get this done. You know what it's like to get in this position.' He looked from Provost to Skinner.

'Give me the two hundred,' Provost said at last.

There was a quick delivery of paper money.

'Don't you have any gold?' Provost suggested.

'Not tonight.'

Provost nodded. 'All right. Tomorrow at the same time. Here.'

Barnes nodded, with a tight grin. The poise he had walked in with was slowly returning. He felt confident all had gone well. 'Tomorrow. Same time.' He glanced at Skinner and Icepick. 'Nice to meet up with you boys.'

There was no reaction.

A couple of minutes later he was gone from the place. Skinner turned to Provost. 'I don't get it. You'll never see that two-bit hustler again.'

Provost turned to Icepick. 'Get

going, and don't lose him. We've discussed this. Make it a secluded place and use the Bowie.'

Icepick hurried after Barnes and disappeared outside. Slowly Skinner turned back to Provost and gave him a knowing grin.

'Now that's the Frank Provost we all know and respect.'

Then he poured Provost and himself another whiskey.

3

O'Brien had been given a small cabin to live in just outside of town by his old partner Smith. The whole structure consisted of one large room that served as kitchen, bedroom, and living quarters. It had been a hunter's cabin at one time, and was quite primitive. It had rough-board floors, which was considered a luxury when it was built, and translucent animal skins stretched over its two windows. The hinges on its only door were heavy leather.

The cabin hadn't been lived in for years when O'Brien came to town, and he himself had only set foot in it to look it over. He expected to move in after this trapping trip with Smith; Sarah Carter had volunteered to clean it up for him before his arrival back in Fort Revenge.

On the morning that O'Brien and

Smith were heading back to town prematurely after their run-in with the gambler from Tulsa, Sarah was out at O'Brien's new home with Abigail Pritchard, who had insisted on helping Sarah in her clean-up job there. Abigail worked for Mayor Spencer with Sarah, and lived at Mrs Barstow's boarding-house where Sarah had a room.

It was a beautiful June day. It had been an enjoyable buggy ride out there, with the redolence of desert blossoms brought to them on a gentle breeze. It would have been a light-hearted time, but for the recent visit of Frank Provost, which had scared both women, the memory of which still lurked at the back of their minds, like bats swooping about, shadow-like, in a dark cave.

Now they were hard at work in the cabin, sweeping the rough floor, dusting ancient surfaces. Sarah hung small curtains at the two windows and hoped they didn't offend O'Brien. She knew that any accommodation superior to a ground blanket in a hardship camp was considered unnecessary luxury by the hunter, who had been known to eschew the use of a bed and sleep on the floor of the room at a seldom-patronized hotel.

'Do you need some help with those curtains, dear?' Abigail asked her from the front of the big room.

'I think I'm just about done.' Sarah smiled at her. When Sarah smiled, her whole face lit up and she was beautiful for a moment, not just pretty.

'I hope you know what you're doing, girl,' Abigail offered. Her grayish hair slightly disheveled from her work, she reopened the heavy wooden door and did some final sweeping-out while Sarah straightened a curtain over a window.

Sarah was a young woman of just over thirty, with long dark hair that at the moment was caught up in a bun at the back of her head, with ringlets of it falling over the sides of her face. She had lovely green eyes in a chiseled face and a trim, very attractive figure that filled out her clothing with curves. She wore a plain gingham dress under an apron.

A couple of months ago she had been living life as a Boston librarian, with two failed romances behind her and a seemingly dismal future. She had become so disillusioned with her life that she had impetuously answered an ad for mail-order brides in the Oklahoma Territory.

Abigail closed the door and wiped at her brow. 'Well, it's beginning to look almost habitable in here.'

Sarah stepped down from a stool, and moved back to admire her handiwork. 'I hope he likes it. I'll make up the bed the last thing.'

Abigail went over to her. 'Are you sure he'll even use it? He was sleeping down at the depot with drivers before he left here.'

'I think he likes the idea of being put here by himself,' Sarah said. She removed the apron and revealed the fullness of her figure. 'He's a loner, you know.'

Abigail gestured toward a crude table and chairs at the center of the room. 'Let's take a rest, honey.'

'Well, we're almost done. But all right.'

They sat at the table, and Sarah reached over and touched Abigail's hand. 'Thanks for riding out here with me,' she said. 'I needed the company.' Abigail was Sarah's only female friend at Fort Revenge so far.

'I'm glad you came here, dear. You make this town seem almost civilized.'

'I'd never have gotten here without O'Brien,' Sarah said soberly. 'And he saved me again when we got here. You remember Jake Latimer? That no-good thief was going to bed me whether or not I married him.'

Abigail looked serious. 'You never told me how you met that trail man.'

Sarah looked across the room, remembering. 'I'd taken passage on a Conestoga. My drivers were murdered by Pawnee while I was out of sight at a stream. I was left alone out there, Abigail. I thought it was just a matter of time before it was over for me. Then O'Brien came along. I've never been so glad to see another face in my life. He brought me here. Reluctantly. Against his better judgement. I owe him, Abigail. And — it's more than that.'

Abigail eyed her studiedly. 'How much more?'

Sarah returned her gaze. 'I don't know. I just know I've never felt so safe with any other man. He puts me at ease, knowing I can count on him absolutely. I guess he would be that way with any friend.'

'From what I hear, he has no friends. Except Smith.'

'As I said, he's a loner,' Sarah said a little defensively. 'He doesn't trust other people easily. But I think if he likes you, he would give his life for you. That's the kind of man he is.'

'Does he like you?' Abigail smiled at her.

Sarah returned it. 'I believe so.'

'Do you want it to be more than that?'

Sarah gave her a mock frown. 'I think I know now why you wanted to sit down and talk.'

Abigail sighed. 'You're my friend, Sarah. Forgive me if I invade your privacy. It's just that I've talked some to Smith about the hunter.'

Sarah held her look silently.

'Smith has known O'Brien since he was a young man. O'Brien has never taken a wife, never even lived with a woman. I get the idea it was a rarity when he even patronized a saloon girl. He just doesn't seem to need a woman in his life, Sarah. He's only half-civilized. He hardly ever sleeps in a bed with a roof over his head. The only men he's ever befriended, besides a couple of other hunters, are Lakota Indians. The Lakota are convinced he emerged full-grown from a bear cave near Ogallala. He's a savage. Maybe he never will be able to live comfortably with us regular humans.'

Sarah's pretty face had grown somber through that summary. 'Abigail, I rode with O'Brien for days on our way here.

We were together day and night. Riding. Eating. Sleeping. He saved me from a bear. Indians tried to buy me and he risked his life to deny them. I know more about O'Brien than anybody here except Smitty. And I can assure you he's not a savage. He was a perfect gentleman with me all the way here. And a friend. So please don't try to tell me about him. You don't know him.'

Abigail sighed. 'I'm sorry. I should have kept quiet about it. It's just that I like you so much. I don't want to see you disappointed.'

'You know what, Abigail? When I was in Boston, I would have worried about getting hurt. But my journey down here, and the adventures I've lived through, have made me a different woman. I've found some inner strength, Abigail. I'm a western woman now, even though I'm still a tenderfoot. In other words, I can take care of myself.'

Abigail nodded. 'I hear you, dear. Just forget I said anything.'

'You're a good friend,' Sarah told her.

'You were just trying to take care of me. Thanks. And now, I think we should get that bunk made up and get back to town to get some work done that we actually get paid for.'

Abigail touched her arm. 'I'll drive this time,' she smiled.

* * *

O'Brien and Smith arrived in town in mid-afternoon, and were surprised to see a long-ago closed-down saloon reopened right across the street from the Prairie Café. They reined in on the dusty street and stared at the sign outside that read, OPEN. A second one announced: GAMING AVAILABLE.

'I'll be damned,' Smith grunted out. 'Thatcher said he might do this. Own two going concerns right across from each other. I think he come into some money in December. Some uncle passed away.'

O'Brien shook his shaggy head. 'That will be a magnet for men like this

Provost. It could change the whole character of the town.'

Smith sighed. 'Come on, let's see how things are going at the depot.'

They rode on down the street a short distance to the Territorial Express depot, the company's headquarters. Smith looked tired. 'I'll take the animals out back and unload the pelts,' O'Brien told his friend. They had brought back just under two dozen beaver and fox pelts, which they would sell at a trading post located to the north just off the stage trail. The pelts would bring a small amount of cash but O'Brien was disappointed with his first venture of that kind in the area.

When O'Brien entered the depot and walked up front to the large waiting room, Smith was on a bench for passengers and talking with two drivers, Ed Reece and a thin, emaciated-looking fellow called Cinch Bug Bailey. He was the one who had been absent that night when Provost's gang came into the café. He was younger than Old Scratch, but looked equally incompetent. He wore a Remington Army .44 high on his belt, and O'Brien doubted seriously if he knew how to use it. Bailey and Reece were talking with Smith animatedly. They all fell silent when the hunter came up to them. His presence seemed to change the feeling in the room.

'The skins are unloaded,' O'Brien said in his deep voice. After that physical work and the long ride to town, he appeared the same as when he had risen from his groundsheet at dawn that morning. 'They'll need a second scraping.'

Smith nodded. 'You know Reece and Bailey. Reece has been filling me in on Frank Provost's visit here.'

'He looks like a man who takes what he wants,' Reece said. 'And I think he wants this whole damn town.'

'Funk said his man Latham took a fancy to Sarah Carter, too,' Bailey grinned.

O'Brien turned slowly to him and just stared.

Smith glanced at O'Brien's square, sober face. 'Well, who wouldn't,' he said in his loud voice.

There were no passengers waiting for a stage at that time, and Funk and Old Scratch were off on a run up north. A heavy silence fell into the room with just the four men sitting quietly. O'Brien finally sat down near Smith on the same bench.

'What's this about Provost wanting the Express?'

Reece nodded. 'He mentioned that specifically. Said it was his main interest. Guess he always wanted to own a stage line.'

'That don't set well in my craw,' Smith said angrily. 'We're going to have to deal with this boy.'

'And with Thatcher opening up that saloon,' O'Brien said, 'within a year men like Provost could swarm here thick as buffalo gnats in August.' He folded his hands on his knees. 'I been thinking on our ride in. I heard of this Provost, when I was up in Kansas. He's fast with his gun. And he kills without giving it a second thought. How many was there?'

'Four,' Reece answered. Of the four drivers, he seemed the most able. He was the youngest of them and could use the Smith & Wesson .32 revolver he carried at all times. 'One of them was scary. Provost called him Icepick and he carried a Bowie as well as his sidearm. He had this dull look in his eyes, you know? Like he ain't all there.'

'And Provost said he wants to pay for the Express?' Smith asked.

'That's what he said. You can imagine what he'd offer. With his gun to back it up. We told him you wasn't interested.'

'He wants to run the stage line and the town, too,' O'Brien commented. 'He'll have to be dealt with head-on.'

Smith rose. 'I'm going over to take a look at that new saloon. You want to join me to wet your whistle, partner?'

O'Brien stood up and left with him, his bearded face pensive.

Ben Pritchard was just finishing

nailing up a sign over the entrance, a temporary one that read, STAGE TRAIL SALOON. He climbed off a ladder and greeted the twosome.

'Hello, boys! Good to have you back! Look at my new enterprise!'

'Can you afford to run both of these places?' Smith frowned. 'The food better not suffer at the Prairie.'

'Oh, no. I'll still be cooking over there, gentlemen. But now we got us a real town. A service that will help Fort Revenge get put on the map.'

'That was what was good about it,' O'Brien offered. 'That nobody knew how to find it. Look what happened the other night when somebody did.'

'Oh. Them. Oh, we'll handle them, boys.' A small laugh.

O'Brien had noticed there was a horse picketed outside on a new hitching rail. They all went inside now, and Smith was impressed with what Thatcher had done to refurbish the place. Newly polished mahogany bar, new mirror behind it. Clean floor, polished tables.

The lone customer was a drifter who was just riding through, and had seen the OPEN sign out front. He had emptied two glasses of rye whiskey and was now pounding on the bar.

'Oh, there you are, you little weasel. Get back there and get me a full bottle of your best rum.'

'Sir, you haven't paid for the other drinks yet,' Thatcher said nicely. 'Would you like to settle up first?'

'Settle up? Why, you goddamn worm!' He grabbed Thatcher by the shirt front and shoved him hard against the bar. Then he drew a Colt revolver and stuck it into Thatcher's face, against his nose. 'Now, you go get that bottle, or I'll scatter your brains all over them shelves back there.'

O'Brien walked over to him casually. He didn't have his Winchester with him, so was unarmed except for the skinning knife in his boot.

'Put him down,' his hard, low voice came to the drifter.

The fellow was almost O'Brien's

height, and tough-looking. He turned hostilely toward the hunter, and his face lost some of its ferocity, but not all. He turned the revolver on O'Brien.

'Butt out of it, trail man,' he said, in a deep growl.

'You ought to listen to him, stranger,' Smith said quietly from down the bar.

'Barkeep, tell your undertaker to pound up a pine coffin,' the drifter said gutturally. His finger went white over the trigger.

But at that same moment O'Brien's left hand shot out and caught the other man's gunhand, shoving the muzzle of the Colt aside as it fired explosively past O'Brien's ear, the lead clanging off a hanging lamp behind O'Brien and ricocheting around the room harmlessly. O'Brien squeezed down on the gunhand with a vice-like grip, and bones cracked audibly as the drifter screamed out in raw pain. The gun fell to the floor, and O'Brien's right fist came smashing into the drifter's face, fracturing his nose and jaw. The drifter went flying off his feet, arms flung wide, crashing over two tables as the splintered and broken remains went to the floor with him. His leg kicked at the newly swept floorboards once, and he was still.

Thatcher stared wide-eyed, and then uttered a low whistle, trying to grasp what had just happened. 'Is he dead?' he whispered.

'He'll live,' Smith told him. 'He might have to eat through a straw for a while.'

O'Brien walked up to the bar, rubbing his right hand. 'Make it two whiskeys,' he growled out. 'And they're on you.'

Smith grinned. 'He's been in a bad mood all day,' he quipped.

4

Almost a thousand miles north on that same afternoon, Ezra Logan and his gunfighter grandson Matt arrived in a small town called Beal's Crossing in north Kansas.

Ezra was feeling his age, and a proposed long journey on horseback like this wore on his old bones. He began wishing he had brought a buggy, or even taken a stagecoach most of the way and tethered their mounts behind it.

But his age hadn't affected his gunplay much. As fast and good as Matt had become with his Iver-Johnson, Ezra was still almost that dangerous with the heavy Tranter .38 that hung on his gunbelt. Ezra was still tough physically too, and nobody in his family had ever challenged his patriarchal position.

Ezra and Matt had taken a bed at a small, unkempt boarding-house on the town's main street, after leaving their mounts with the local hostler. They had had a barely edible meal in the nearby dining room, but wolfed it down like it was their last on death row, they had both been so hungry. Now they sat on a short sofa in a parlor for guests, Ezra smoking a Cuban cigar and blowing smoke rings into the air. It was almost dark outside.

'This beats the trail,' Ezra was saying through the smoke. 'I might stay here a coupla nights.'

There was just one other person in the room, a gray-haired woman reading a book in an easy chair across the room. She looked up at Ezra with a frown.

'We don't want to waste too much time,' Matt said to Ezra. 'The sooner we find that — ' He glanced over at the woman. 'That hunter, the sooner we can deliver our important message to him.'

The woman called across the room.

'There's no smoking in the lounge, sir. It's house rules.'

Ezra's weathered face grew a smile. He looked at his cigar as if studying its smoke-emitting capability. 'Are you bothered by good cigar smoke, lady?'

'I can smell that foul odor clear over here!' she exclaimed.

Ezra rose and walked over to her. 'You know what? I'll wager a half-eagle that if you took just one puff of this fine cigar, you'd get a liking for the smell. How about it?' He held the cigar close to her nose.

Frightened, she rose quickly, huffing, and almost ran from the room.

Ezra laughed loudly. Matt just shook his head. 'You want to get us kicked out of here, Ezra?'

'That would take about six armed men,' Ezra grinned, and went back to the sofa, blowing another smoke ring. In that moment, an older man walked into the parlor, middle-aged and wearing a buckskin shirt over dungaree trousers. His Stetson was crumpled and trail-dusty. He sat on a chair not far away.

'Boys,' he nodded to them. Then he opened up a Kansas City newspaper.

Ezra looked him over. 'Say, would you be a hunter, mister?'

The other man looked up at him expressionless. 'You talking to me?'

Ezra nodded, leaning forward on the sofa. 'I saw your rawhides. You a buffalo hunter?'

The other man put the paper down. 'When I can find them. Right now they're as scarce as bankers in heaven.'

Ezra gave a little laugh at the comment as an ash fell off his cigar on to the oriental carpet. 'How long you been doing it? Buffalo hunting?'

The stranger frowned slightly. 'You one of them reporters?' he said, acidly.

Ezra laughed louder. 'I reckon you got to be able to read to be one of them boys.'

'If it's important to you, I been at it quite a spell,' the man told him.

'Well, we're on the trail of a boy who

74

used to do the same thing,' Ezra went on. 'Maybe you met him. The name is O'Brien.'

The hunter folded the paper, and studied Ezra's face. 'How is it you know O'Brien?'

'Then you do know him,' Ezra persisted.

'We met him up in Colorado,' Matt blurted out quickly.

Ezra gave his grandson a dark look. 'Yeah. He had a cabin in the mountains.'

The hunter nodded. 'I heard that. Why are you looking for him?'

Ezra hesitated. 'Some relative of his left him some money. We been appointed to find him and let him know.'

The hunter narrowed his eyes slightly. 'I didn't know he had any relatives.'

Ezra gave a laugh. 'Well, he might not know about this one. That's the idea we got. Right, Matt?'

Matt hesitated. 'Yeah. That's right.'

'We heard he come through here lately. I reckon you ain't seen him?'

'Can't say I have,' the hunter said. 'Used to see him regular at the Missoula Rendezvous. And at Big Bend. He always had the best pelts of all the hunters. I heard he give it up for trapping.'

'You know, we heard the same thing!' Ezra said nicely.

'The same thing,' Matt echoed him.

Another irritated look. 'Did you know him personally?' Ezra then pursued.

'I've talked with him some. He never spent much time palavering. Some hunters called him ornery. But never to his face.'

'I see,' Ezra mused. 'So he could handle hisself pretty good, then?'

The hunter frowned again. 'What's that have to do with giving him money?'

Ezra tried a stiff smile. 'Oh, it's just an old man's curiosity.'

The hunter unfolded the paper. 'Well, I can tell you one thing: you didn't want to cross him. He treated other traders fair, and expected to be treated the same way. He dealt a lot with Indians. I think he growed up among them in the Shenandoah.'

'Good with a gun?' Ezra said.

The hunter's frown deepened. 'He don't carry. Calls sidearms pea-shooters. But I hear he can hit a buffalo in the eye at a quarter-mile with that Sharps Big Fifty he uses. Day or night.'

Matt looked over at Ezra, who just sat there for a moment. 'Ain't you stretching the blanket just a little bit there, boy?'

The hunter shrugged. 'I never seen it. I'm just telling you what I heard. But knowing him just a little, I'd believe it.'

The hunter went back to his paper then and, after a moment, Ezra rose and left the room with Matt just behind him. They went out on to the empty front porch of the house together. Ezra flipped the cigar stub on to the ground as they stood looking out into the blackness. The end of the cigar glowed down there in the darkness.

'So he can hit a damn shaggy with a buffalo gun at a distance. I ain't no buffalo and I expect to be right behind him.'

Matt looked over at him. 'He don't even carry a sidearm. I can put three in him before he can find the trigger on a rifle.'

Ezra met his grandson's look. 'Maybe you better get this straight, boy. This ain't going to be no fast-draw contest. We're not going to take the slightest chance of messing this up. We're going to come up behind that rattlesnake some dark night and put enough lead in him to swamp-sink him even before he can turn around. Then we'll turn him over and make him look into the faces of the Logans who put him in his grave.'

Young Matt nodded. 'That suits me right down to the ground.'

⋆　⋆　⋆

O'Brien slept at the depot that first night back. The next morning was warm and sunny. Smith kept a private room for himself in the depot, which was his only living quarters at the moment. He prefered living there over being isolated out at the cabin he had given O'Brien. But for O'Brien, who had little interest in sleeping with drivers at the rear of the depot, the cabin filled a need.

When Smith came around with a hot cup of coffee for O'Brien at eight, O'Brien had been up for two hours, taken a walk down to the hostelry to curry his Appaloosa, and returned back to make up his bunk.

'Here. Put this down,' Smith said, giving O'Brien the coffee. 'It'll pry the sleep out of your eyes, partner.'

'That happened two hours ago,' O'Brien told him, downing half the cup in one long swig. 'But that does go down good. When I was on the street earlier, I noticed the saloon was open already and there was two mounts tethered outside. Every damn drifter who used to ride right through here will stop for drinks now. And if Provost comes back it will be a perfect place to work from. I don't know what Thatcher was thinking.'

'Well, maybe it will give the company some business,' Smith observed. He sat on a bunk next to O'Brien's. Over in a corner, R.C. Funk was snoring lightly. 'What are we going to do about this Provost, O'Brien?'

Before O'Brien could respond, Sarah Carter came through the doorway to the front part of the building, carrying a covered dish of food. 'Oh, good!' she said, in a warm, melodious voice. 'I thought I'd catch you two here.'

They just stared at her. Her dark hair was down on her shoulders, and her green eyes were alight with her bouyant personality. She was the prettiest thing either man had ever looked at.

'Well, I'll be bull-whipped!' Smith roared out. 'If that ain't a picture to paint!'

'I thought you two needed some decent food your first morning back.'

Sarah smiled radiantly. She handed the dish to O'Brien, and he took it with a quizzical look. 'Yours is still on the buggy, Smitty,' she added.

Smith gave O'Brien a wry smile. 'I'll just go fetch it,' he said.

Sarah sat down on O'Brien's bunk beside him, which made his blood pressure shoot up and his throat go a little dry. He was unnecessarily embarrassed by his quick emotional response to her. It had been the same ever since he had found her sitting alone out there on the prairie, under a white parasol. He had never seen a woman who looked like her, or talked like her, and he recognized her as special. But it unnerved him that he got this rush of emotional reaction whenever she was near him. It made him feel vulnerable, a feeling he had never known in his entire life.

She reached over and removed the dish cover, and brushed against him.

'It's ham and eggs,' she said. 'And still warm. You start on it while I go take a look at Smitty's bills of lading.'

O'Brien nodded. 'Looks good, Sarah. Thanks.'

By the time Sarah had added up some bills of lading for Smith, and checked some other paperwork, the two men had finished eating and found Sarah at Smith's small office up front.

'Thanks for the grub, Sarah,' Smith told her. 'We probably wouldn't have got over to the café this morning. Anyway, Thatcher is probably taking care of customers over at his new saloon.'

'I was sorry to see that open up,' she admitted. 'Men act differently when they get some liquor in them.'

'Especially some men,' O'Brien offered.

Sarah frowned slightly. 'Why didn't you sleep at your cabin last night? Abigail and I fixed it all up for you. I can't wait till you see it.'

'I just wanted to lay my head down on the nearest thing,' O'Brien said. 'But I expect to go out there tonight.'

'Oh, do you mind if I go with you? To show you everything we did? It would give me so much pleasure!'

O'Brien regarded her silently for a moment, then smiled behind his trimmed beard. His smiles were treasured by Smith because they were so rare. The hunter was a hard-bitten survivor of a thousand misadventures on the trail, a man who had learned to mistrust other men, and who had had few reasons to give his smiling approval of the world around him.

'I reckon that would be fine,' he answered Sarah quietly. 'I'm heading out there at sunset.'

'We'll go in my buggy,' she offered. 'You can tie the Appaloosa behind. I'll be through at Mayor Spencer's by then. You can pick me up there.'

O'Brien liked to hear Sarah talk. He had never known an educated person before. And this one a librarian. O'Brien had never seen the inside of a library. His reading ability was rudimentary, and Sarah had promised to teach him to read as soon as they were settled in at Fort Revenge. He hadn't rejected the offer, but he had no intention of accepting it.

'I'll see you there,' he told her.

He helped her up on to her buggy outside when she left, and felt a heat burgeon inside him when he did. He pushed it back, not wanting to acknowledge it.

When she was gone, Smith came out and gave O'Brien a sly grin. 'I saw your face when you touched her. Maybe it's getting through that thick head what a lucky bastard you really are.'

O'Brien turned a grave look on him. 'You never elbowed your way into my private affairs when we rode together, Smitty; don't start now.' Then he walked back inside to get some work done on the drivers' schedules.

It was just shortly before the sun dipped below the distant buttes in the west that O'Brien stopped at the mayor's house to get Sarah. Spencer invited O'Brien inside while Sarah was tidying up for the drive, and they stood inside the door while Spencer spoke to him in a lowered voice.

'I guess you know by now about that Tulsa gang that was in here.'

O'Brien nodded. 'What can you tell me about them?'

'They were four tough-looking men. Actually, Provost himself was quite civilized-acting. Didn't really threaten, just talked about investing here. It was the men with him who worried me. He called one Icepick. Scary-looking fellow with a tic that jerks at his mouth. The one called Latham has this eye. You can't tell where he's looking. The third one looked to be his main man. Tough. Brawny. When Provost talks, they listen. They all looked like they knew how to use the guns they carried. If they come back, I think they could be real trouble.'

Before O'Brien could reply, Sarah came into the room, bright and cheery. 'I'm ready, O'Brien. Let's take a look at the cabin.'

It was a warm, dusty ride out there. There were pencil streaks of crimson along the horizon where the sun had just set, but there was plenty of light left in the sky. O'Brien helped Sarah off the buggy at the cabin and then he entered it for the first time since his arrival in Fort Revenge.

He stopped stock-still in the door-way.

Sarah was just ahead of him, and looked back in surprise. Then alarm. 'You don't like it.'

O'Brien stepped on into the big room, with its swept floors, window curtains, and air of order. 'Uh. No, it's real nice, Sarah. Just like walking into a Kansas City hotel room.'

'Oh, dear. You really don't like it.'

He turned to her. 'Would you relax? I mean it, this will be just fine.' He had brought his saddle-bags off the horse with him, and he walked over slowly to the made-up bunk, and threw them on to it. 'Just fine.'

'I can take the curtains down if you like the windows plain.'

He threw his Stetson on to the bunk, too, and then came and took her arms into his thick hands, and she felt a little thrill ripple through her. 'You did a real nice job. Would you quit fretting about it? You're skittery as a buffalo calf under sheet lightning.'

Sarah smiled at that comparison. 'Sorry. I just wanted everything to be right. It's your new home.'

He held her for a moment, feeling the electricity crackling silently between them. When he released her, she was breathing shallowly.

'It will be good, just knowing you done all this,' he said eventually. He felt awkward, and went and looked into a small fireplace across the room which Sarah and Abigail had also cleaned out. 'The flue looks clear. I can boil my coffee there.' He turned to her again. 'Can I make you a cup? I see there's some goods on that shelf over there.'

'No, thanks,' she answered, getting her composure back. She had nursed him back to health after a shooting incident when he first arrived in town, and he had begun treating her differently after that. Riding together all the way there from Kansas, he had been barely civil to her. 'I'll be having dinner later,' she added.

'Well,' he said quietly. 'I'm much

obliged you coming out here like this. I'll see you to your buggy.'

He didn't notice the disappointment on her face. 'Oh. All right.'

They walked outside together, and O'Brien unhitched the Appaloosa and tethered it to a short hitching post in front of the cabin. It was dark outside now, and a full moon hung brightly over their heads. O'Brien shaded his eyes and looked into the distance.

'I didn't know the old fort was so close,' he said. 'You can see it plain in the moonlight.'

Sarah followed his gaze, and saw the black silhouette of the old Indian fort for which the town was named. 'Oh! What a lovely sight at night!' she exclaimed. 'You know, I haven't been out to the old fort yet.'

He had already helped her aboard the buggy. He looked up at her now. 'I'll drive you over there if you want. Before you head back to town.'

She gave him a beautiful smile that made his mouth go slightly dry. 'Why,

'I'd love that, O'Brien.' She knew his Welsh first name, but on their way to Fort Revenge he had admonished her never to use it, and she didn't.

O'Brien climbed aboard the buggy, took the reins, and nudged the dun mare forward along a bumpy track to the fort. They arrived just moments later, and he reined in just in front of the fort's big gateway.

The stockade gate was gone, as was much of the fort wall, scavenged by area farmers and ranchers for use in their buildings. They could see inside the compound, and it had a ghostly, eerie quality.

'I love it,' she said quietly.

O'Brien nodded. 'I guess they did a lot of trading here, too,' he offered. 'After the shooting was over.'

'Was there shooting?'

'The Kiowa didn't like settlers here,' he said. He paused. 'I reckon you can't blame them.'

Off in the near distance came the sound of a coyote howling at the sky.

'That's a beautiful sound. We heard it

on the trail coming here from Kansas. It was new to me then.'

'He's howling at the full moon,' O'Brien told her. 'It does something to them. Smitty and me used to call it the coyote moon, the full one. Sometimes the night was just loud with that sound. And it would go all night.' He gazed up at the moon, as his voice trailed off.

Sarah observed him soberly. 'You miss it already, don't you?'

O'Brien sat there silently for a long moment. 'It gets in a man's blood, Sarah. But you have to change with the times. I know that. The West will never be like it was again. That world is gone forever. Now there's just room for towns and farms and stage lines and drivers' schedules.' He sighed. 'Don't take no mind of me, though. I always been all right with change. I'll make it.'

'I know you will,' Sarah said softly, wishing she could reach out and put an arm around him. But he was like a wild coyote. If you pushed too hard, it would disappear and you would never see it again. 'Maybe we ought to get back now,' she added.

A few minutes later, O'Brien was situating the Appaloosa under a shelter behind the cabin and Sarah was halfway back to town.

★　★　★

At eight the next morning, the Territorial Express stagecoach dusted off on its Tulsa run, with Old Scratch driving and Reece riding shotgun. Eight passengers left with them: six local residents and two travelers coming through from the north. Smith had been busy getting the stage ready, and giving the drivers last-minute instructions. O'Brien was drawing up a new schedule for drivers and stage, and his illiteracy slowed him way down and frustrated him. Partway through the job, he broke a pencil in half and threw it violently across the room, swearing under his breath, and went out back to air some mattresses. Smith found him there.

'Where's the new schedule? I want to post it.'

'It's in that waste bucket up there,' O'Brien grumbled. 'I can't spell the damn days of the week.' He pounded dust out of a mattress with a big fist. 'And I ain't aiming to learn, by Jesus,' he growled, not looking at Smith.

Smith frowned, then sighed. 'I should have remembered. You can talk with savages in five languages but can't hardly sign your own name. This is on me, partner. Listen. Sarah comes in three times a week to help with record-keeping. You tell her what schedule you want, and let her write it all down on paper. That ain't man's work, anyhow.'

O'Brien gave him a look. 'I don't need no damn help,' he gritted. He was very embarrassed, a feeling he despised. 'I'll figure it out. I might ride shotgun for a while. You ain't got nobody here who can actually use a gun if it's needed.'

'That's a good idea,' Smith agreed quickly. 'Get your feet wet, so to speak.

Learn the business from the bottom. But I'll be wanting your management advice right soon, partner. I'm thinking we could use a second stagecoach and start another whole route going east and west. There's crossroads villages in both directions, and we could pick up some ranch trade.'

O'Brien sat down on one of the bunks used by drivers. 'Smitty, I know I bought in, and I know I told you I'd help you get this outfit running good, but I don't know if this is for me. I'm going to have to do some hard thinking on this over the next few weeks. I'll end up going out trapping all the time and leaving the company work here for you. I wouldn't want that.'

'Hell, just having your cash investment was a godsend. If I had nothing more than that and you riding shotgun that would be enough.'

'We'll talk more on it later,' O'Brien told him. 'And I'll have that schedule for you later today.'

They both looked up as Mayor

Spencer came striding through the depot to where they now stood in the bunk room. 'There you are!' Spencer called out. 'I hoped I'd find you both here.' He clapped Smith on his heavy shoulder. 'We haven't really talked about this Provost thing. Have you boys given it any thought?'

Smith shrugged. 'Provost ain't exactly a priority here, Mayor. We got a stage line to run.'

'He made it pretty clear he was coming back to Fort Revenge,' Spencer went on. 'And you boys have the only dependable armed men in town. We'll be looking to you if there's trouble.'

'Our drivers would be more dangerous to themselves than to Provost if they tried to use their guns,' O'Brien grunted out. 'Reece is the only one who knows where to find a trigger assembly. We'll deal with Provost if and when he shows up again.'

Spencer looked from O'Brien to Smith, and Smith shrugged. 'That makes sense, Mayor.'

'I think it's about time we hired us a lawman here,' Spencer said heavily. 'I could place an ad in the Tulsa newspaper.'

Smith laughed in his throat. 'That would bring every gunfighter in a hundred miles to try for the job.'

'The man who tried to steal my hides up in Colorado was a so-called lawman,' O'Brien commented. 'Hell, Wyatt Earp over in Tombstone used to hold up stages for a living. I don't trust any man who carries iron to make his way.'

Spencer eyed him closely. 'Have you ever thought of pinning a badge on?'

O'Brien gave him a hard look. 'Do I look like a gun-fighter to you?'

'O'Brien prefers to enforce rules his own way,' Smith grinned.

'Well,' Spencer said, 'you just look like the type that could get the job done. You could do it and still keep on with the stage line, you know.'

O'Brien threw a mattress on to the floor and turned to him. 'Are you hard of hearing, Mayor?'

Spencer's face colored slightly, and he sputtered out a response. 'I meant no offense, O'Brien.'

O'Brien picked a mattress up from a bunk and took it outside, not paying Spencer any further attention. Smith gave Spencer an embarrassed smile.

'Sorry, Mayor. He ain't really been town-trained yet.'

Spencer shook his head. 'I'm not accustomed to people speaking to me quite like that. Are you sure he'll be any help if we have trouble here?'

The smile faded off Smith's beefy face. 'Mr Mayor, mark my word: that boy will do to tie to. If trouble comes, he'll stand his ground till Hell freezes over and then skate some on the ice.' A small grin.

Spencer smiled uncertainly, and looked outside where O'Brien was hanging the mattress on a fence post. 'Well, no offense intended. I'll talk to you later.'

Smith spat through the doorway into the dust outside. 'Looking forward, Mayor.'

O'Brien did eventually finish the

paperwork on the schedules that afternoon, and shortly thereafter found Smith sweeping off the porch outside the front entrance of the depot. Smith turned and saw him, and pointed to thunderclouds off in the west.

'Looks like we'll get some weather tonight.'

O'Brien scanned the horizon. 'It'll blow over by morning.'

'Remember that time on the Brazos? Tracking that herd so big you couldn't see all the way through it? We had a big one that night. That storm was a gully-washing, fence-post-raising toad strangler.'

'That country was all catclaw and prickly pear,' O'Brien said. 'Dry country. You spit and it come out dust.'

'We had to share that hunt with a couple of others,' Smith reminisced. 'Some guy named Watts was one. Didn't know how to stake a buff out to skin it.'

'If that boy had dynamite for brains,' O'Brien remembered, 'he couldn't blow the top of his head off.'

Smith laughed a booming laugh. 'And clumsy as a pig on stilts!' he barked out, choking a bit at the end. He looked over at O'Brien, and O'Brien caught his gaze. They stared at each other silently.

'I'm going to take a couple days off from office work,' O'Brien said. 'Think I'll ride shotgun tomorrow morning with Funk. On the Tulsa run.'

Smith frowned. 'Fine. But why Tulsa?'

O'Brien gave him an acid look. 'I ain't going looking for Provost. I just need a break from this.'

'Well, keep out of trouble. I need you. Funk is picking up a small payroll from a new bank we made contact with. And I expect you'll have return passengers. Try not to scare them.'

O'Brien sighed. 'You really are a pain in the butt sometimes, partner. I'll try not to ruin your good reputation.'

That evening O'Brien walked to the Prairie Café alone, since Smith had had Mrs Barstow bring him a bowl of soup earlier and wanted nothing else. When O'Brien entered the place he was surprised to find Sarah and Abigail Pritchard sitting together. They usually took their meals at Mrs Barstow's rooming-house where they both lived. There were other customers there, and just one empty table in a corner. Before O'Brien could figure out what to do, Sarah saw him.

'O'Brien! Over here!'

O'Brien walked over to them reluctantly. He tipped his Stetson. 'Ladies.' He looked big, rugged and masculine, standing over them. Abigail was slightly intimidated by his proximity.

'We're still eating.' Sarah smiled widely at him. Her hair was caught up behind her head in a twist, with remnants cascading down her cheeks. Her radiant face looked beautiful to him, and he tried not to show it. 'Why don't you join us?'

O'Brien would rather have been run over by stampeding buffalo than sit at that table with two women. 'Well, I was heading for that empty table at the back of the room.'

Abigail had regained her presence of mind. 'Nonsense. You must sit with us, Mr O'Brien. You'd be lonely back there.' She gave Sarah a knowing smile.

O'Brien had begun carrying his Winchester under his arm again, now that the saloon had opened across the street. 'All right, ma'am,' he said, as if receiving a sentence in court. He seated himself at the table, and leaned the rifle against it, beside him. Abigail noticed it for the first time, and gasped slightly.

'Are you enjoying the cabin now?' Sarah asked. Whenever she was near him, she felt an uncontrollable emotion build inside her, a pleasant excitement she had never felt before in her life. She kept telling herself to ignore it, that it was unimportant, but she knew on some level it wasn't, and that worried her: the hunter showed no evidence of similar feelings.

'It's right comfortable, Sarah,' he said. 'And thank you, too, Mrs Pritchard, for your help.' She felt the presence of him like a powerful force in the room, and

100

when she spoke, it was with shallow breaths.

'You're quite welcome, of course,' she breathed out.

The owner, Thatcher, came over to the table in his apron. 'Ah, O'Brien. Sitting with the ladies. What can I get for you?'

O'Brien cast a scowl at him that evaporated the stiff smile. 'Did you make up some stew today?'

'Yes, sir. Very tasty it is, too.'

'Bring me a bowl. And I'm buying the ladies' meals, too.'

Thatcher disappeared, and Sarah and Abigail made some small talk with O'Brien, who participated with nods and grunts. Two men came in and walked to the empty table at the rear, not far away. They both wore guns, and had obviously just come from Thatcher's saloon across the street. They looked around the room, their glances stopping on O'Brien's table. They made some whispered comments between them, which O'Brien didn't see.

Thatcher came out with O'Brien's stew, and O'Brien and the women continued eating, with Sarah doing most of the talking about the stage-line business. The two men ordered steaks, and then Thatcher was gone again.

'I ain't much good at paperwork,' O'Brien was saying to Sarah. 'I try to keep busy with other stuff.'

Once again, his open vulnerability touched Sarah, and she felt the strong urge again to hug him, smother him with her affection, reassure him. 'You'll get on to it,' she said encouragingly. 'It just takes time.'

They were all about finished eating now. Other customers had left the place, and there was just a lone man in another corner, them, and the newcomers.

'Hey, mister! You a buffalo hunter?' called one of the two men, the taller of the two. He had a pock-marked lower face and slitted, narrow eyes. His companion was heavy-set and jowly in the face. It was apparent both of them had been drinking.

O'Brien sighed. They hadn't had this sort of thing here before Thatcher opened up his saloon. He looked over at the two, and then back to his stew, which was almost gone. He ladled out a spoonful without responding to the tall man.

'Just ignore them,' Sarah said soberly.

'Hey, are you deaf, mister? Or is it miss, at that table?'

'Mind your own business over there!' Sarah blurted out.

O'Brien turned to her in surprise, and when he saw the fire in those lovely green eyes, he just stared for a moment. Abigail looked very nervous.

'Why don't you ladies go on home now?' he suggested.

The tall drifter called over again. 'I guess you have to let the womenfolk do your talking, hunter!'

Sarah glared at them as she and Abigail rose from their chairs.

'Go on now,' O'Brien said quietly.

Abigail hurried out the door without

looking back. Sarah caught O'Brien's eye. 'Be careful.' Fear in her face now.

He grunted. 'You should've told them that.'

Sarah tried an uncertain smile, and then was gone. The only other customer besides the drifters watched events, breathless, in the far corner. O'Brien grabbed the Winchester where it rested against the table, and turned to the two men.

'Now, I guess you boys wanted to talk.'

The beefy one laughed in his throat. 'What do you reckon to do with that long gun, miss? I don't see no buffalo in here.'

'Maybe he saw a cockroach come in from the kitchen,' the tall one added, joining in the laughter.

'You boys ain't eating them steaks,' O'Brien said softly.

The smiles evaporated. 'Huh?' the beefy one frowned.

'You ain't got the manners to chow down in a civilized place,' O'Brien went on. 'I reckon I'll ask you to leave.'

The two men exchanged a look of disbelief as complete silence fell into the room like a thick prairie fog. The lone customer in the corner swallowed back his growing tension.

The tall drifter rose from his chair. 'You just earned yourself a six-foot hole up at Boot Hill, hunter.' And in the next half-second he went for the revolver on his hip.

O'Brien had seen his intent in his eyes even before he made the move for the gun. In that split second the muzzle of the rifle swung up in a flashing motion and fired just as the tall man was aiming the sidearm to fire. The rifle exploded raucously in the café, the lead smacking into the tall drifter's gunhand and shattering it before he could fire the weapon.

The drifter cried out in pain as the gun clattered to the floor. He stood there holding the bloodied, crushed hand, staring at it in disbelief. O'Brien saw another movement in his peripheral vision, and the beefy drifter was rising, his hand going out over his gun, and drew. He had O'Brien beat. But he looked into O'Brien's eyes at the last moment, hesitated, and holstered the weapon.

'What's the matter?' O'Brien said quietly. 'Maybe your mouth is bigger than that iron you carry.'

'You goddamn animal! Look what you done to my partner!'

'He's lucky he ain't dead,' O'Brien told him. 'Now the two of you vamoose. And I mean now. We like to keep the place clean of trash.'

When O'Brien was gone, Thatcher ventured out carefully from the kitchen, having heard the rifle blast. 'Is everything all right out here?' Then he saw the beefy drifter wrapping his partner's hand with a cloth napkin. 'Oh, Jesus.'

The corner customer was shaking his head. 'Might as well eat them steaks yourself, Thatcher. These boys won't be hungry now.'

5

Sarah was waiting tensely for O'Brien when he arrived back on the street that night. She stood beside a hitching rail, holding her breath till it was over. When he came down to her she impetuously ran to him and threw her arms around his broad shoulders. He let it happen, regarding her curiously. 'Hey. It's OK.'

Her eyes were moist. 'There was that shot. I thought you might be — '

He looked into her teary eyes, embarrassed. 'So you been out here the whole time?'

She released him, and wiped at an eye. 'Sorry. You're not impervious to harm, you know. I nursed you through a gunshot already, remember?'

O'Brien hadn't had anyone worry over him since his Welsh mother in the Shenandoah, and it briefly touched a new and pleasant feeling in him. He got himself together. 'What the hell is 'impervious'?'

'Oh. You know. It could happen again. I don't think I could — '

He put a hand gently on her shoulder, and made a shiver race through her whole body. 'Come on, Sarah. Before they get out here. I'll walk you home.'

★   ★   ★

The next morning the Tulsa stage dusted out of town at just after eight, with Shanghai Smith waving it off from the depot porch. There were four passengers aboard and R.C. Funk was driving. Sitting beside him on the buckboard was O'Brien, riding shotgun.

The trip took most of the morning, but was uneventful. The passengers arrived at the Express depot dusty, fatigued and out of sorts. Funk and O'Brien unloaded their luggage and most of them just carried it to a hotel right next door. One man was transfering to another stage going east.

'You boys drive that thing too fast!' he complained to O'Brien.

'Next time we'll let you drive,' O'Brien responded, picking the fellow's bag up and carrying it into the depot.

Funk grinned in embarrassment. 'You'll like the trip east. Them stages go so slow you'll think you're going backwards sometimes.'

The fellow gave him a sour look and disappeared inside. In a moment O'Brien came back out.

'We don't head home till early tomorrow,' Funk told him. 'Right after the stop at the bank. We'll have a few customers again. I got us a room at that little hotel down the street a coupla blocks.'

O'Brien looked in that direction, and nodded. The street was busy with wagons, carriages and buggies, and there were boardwalks where women strolled with parasols looking in shop windows. It was all a little like an alien planet to O'Brien, who almost never got into a city.

'This will be the whole world pretty soon, won't it?'

'Huh?'

'I'm going to walk the riding kinks out. Is that hotel with the sign out front ours? That says, SILVER NUGGET?'

'That's the one,' Funk said apologetically. 'We don't spend much on accommodations.'

'I'd rather sleep on the ground,' O'Brien commented. 'You take the stage out back and take care of the horses. I'll see you at the hotel later.'

Funk hadn't expected O'Brien to spend any time with him. He already knew O'Brien's reputation. 'Right. Later,' he nodded.

O'Brien walked down the street on the boardwalks, the Winchester under his arm. Two women and one man crossed the street when they saw him coming. He didn't notice. He was looking into shop windows and staring at things he had never seen before. Men's fancy suits and bowlers, women's summer dresses on support stands. Highboy chests with brass accoutrements.

It all made him a little ill.

At the first saloon he came to, he stepped in just to get away from that bizarre world outside, the world that was coming to the Old West.

The saloon he entered was the Staked Plain Saloon, where Provost had met the man who owed him money that night, and that he patronized regularly when in town. O'Brien walked up to the mahogany bar and ordered a Planters' Rye whiskey and downed it in one gulp.

'Do it again, barkeep,' he called out. He laid the rifle on the bar, and caused the bartender a worried look.

Across the room, Icepick Munro and Slim Latham sat nursing a bottle of imported rum. As O'Brien ordered the second drink, Icepick squinted down and studied O'Brien.

'Well, look over there,' he said quietly.

'What?'

'That man in buckskins. I just saw

that Fort Revenge stage rein in down the street when we was coming in.'

'So?' Latham remarked, swigging a shot glass of rum.

'You got clabber for brains, boy? One of the owners of that Express company is a hunter named O'Brien. Provost asked a drifter about him yesterday.' He leaned forward, his black-as-coal eyes glistening in a sallow face. 'If he just got off that stage, that's O'Brien.'

Latham's face had grown a scowl after Icepick's remarks to him. He focused his wandering eye on the thin man. 'Don't bone me, Munro. I ain't no dummy, you know.'

Icepick sighed in disgust. 'Don't you get it? We can talk to him. About them selling the express. Surprise Provost.'

'I ain't sure Frank would like that,' Latham said hostilely. 'Leave me out of it.'

Icepick shrugged. 'Suit yourself. I'll be right back.'

Icepick strutted over to the bar, his Starr .44 hanging low on his hip. He cut

112

a trim, wiry figure as he walked up to the bar very near O'Brien. He ordered a black ale, and when it was delivered, he turned to O'Brien, who was still working on the second whiskey.

'Excuse me, mister,' Icepick said in his high voice. 'Did you just get off that stage down the street?'

O'Brien glanced over at him and looked him over. 'Drink your ale, boy.'

Icepick's face changed, and the tic pulled at his cheek. 'Just trying to be sociable. O'Brien.'

O'Brien took a better look at him. 'Who the hell are you?' He stood two inches taller than Icepick, and was dangerous-looking in his beard and rawhides.

Icepick tried to still the tic, but it jerked at his face again. 'I'm somebody you'll be doing business with pretty soon. I work for Frank Provost.'

O'Brien studied his face more closely.

'That's my partner back there watching us,' Icepick went on. 'Name of Latham.'

O'Brien turned slightly and looked at

Latham, and Latham glanced down at his glass. O'Brien turned back to Icepick. 'So you're the pack of weasels that think you can buy the Express.'

Icepick's face reddened. 'You'll push that saucy line too far, hunter. I come over here friendly-like. I expect to be treated the same.' He hadn't touched the ale.

O'Brien didn't expect to meet any of the Provost gang on his trip to Tulsa. He laid his right hand on the Winchester, but remembered Smith's advice to stay out of trouble while in the city. He sighed. 'I think it was made clear to you already: the Express ain't for sale.'

'You're a hardcase, O'Brien. I reckon we'll have to talk with your partner.'

O'Brien gave him a brittle look. 'Did anybody ever say you look like you been dead for a week with blowflies on your head?'

Icepick's face went red again, and his breath came short. His hand went out over his gun. 'I could blow you full of little round holes before you could move that long gun, mister.'

'Talk's cheap,' O'Brien countered, swigging the rest of his whiskey. He turned and let a steely gaze fall on to Icepick's angry face. 'Now, if you ain't flashing iron, get to hell away from me before I commence on you.'

Icepick's chest was heaving. His right hand grasped the butt of the Starr, but something about the hunter made him hesitate. He swallowed back his anger. 'You and me will talk again,' he growled. 'In Fort Revenge.'

'I hear there's some good doctors in this town,' O'Brien grunted out, tossing some coins on to the bar. 'Maybe they can fix that tic for you, so people won't know when you're about to soil your pants.'

Then he turned his back and left Icepick standing there fuming. He knew he would hear the gunman's draw if he made the move behind him. When he was gone, Icepick saw a slight grin on the bartender's lips. Angrily he threw the entire contents of the ale glass all over the bartender, slammed the glass down on the counter so hard it broke into fragments, then stalked back to his table where Latham was trying to keep a straight face.

★ ★ ★

It was the next morning in Fort Revenge, and hours before O'Brien and Funk were to arrive back from Tulsa, when Sarah Carter arrived at the depot with a bowl of porridge for Smith and Old Scratch, who were alone there. Smith was in his office working on his books, and Old Scratch was out back cleaning up.

'Well, look who's here!' Smith greeted her jovially. He thought Sarah was about the prettiest thing he had ever laid eyes on, and privately hoped O'Brien would come to his senses some day soon and understand how fortunate he was that this breath of spring air from Boston had become enamored of him. He figured it was clear to everybody but O'Brien that Sarah thought the hunter was the best thing that had ever happened to her, when he came upon her out on the prairie that day.

'Good morning, Smitty.' She smiled broadly. She was the only person besides O'Brien that Smith allowed to call him by that name. 'I know how seldom you people eat breakfast down here so thought I'd let you start the day off right this time.' She set one covered dish down. 'I'll just take this back to your driver.'

She was back momentarily, and Smith was already eating.

'Say, this is getting to be a regular thing with you. We'll have to start paying you pretty soon.'

'Mrs Barstow doesn't charge me extra to do this,' she told him. 'Our meal was finished; this would have been thrown out.' She sat down at a chair beside his desk. 'Don't forget, I'll be in tomorrow to help with your books.'

'How could I forget?' he boomed out. He had a full beard, like O'Brien, and he wiped at it with a sleeve. 'It's the high point of the week when you stop in.'

'I understand O'Brien is in Tulsa.'

Smith nodded. 'He had to get away from this. I feel for him, Sarah. Being inside is like prison to him. I got all that out of my system some, but I don't think he ever will. Maybe I made a mistake talking him into a partnership here. I guess I was being a little selfish. I like to have him around.'

'So do I,' Sarah said quietly, staring across the room.

Smith stopped eating, and put his spoon down. 'I apologize if I'm getting too personal here, Sarah,' he started slowly, 'but I think you might be getting serious about that boy.'

Sarah's pretty face colored. 'I'm sorry it's so obvious.'

Smith blew his cheeks out. 'I don't think it's obvious to him. If it was, it would scare him right out of his boots.' He gave a small laugh. 'Sarah, there ain't a man in this territory that wouldn't shoot his mount to win your approval. Except O'Brien. He's never let anybody close to him, except me and maybe one other hunter, back when. He's never placed any value on womenfolk, since his folks was all took down with the diphtheria when he was just a kid. But I have to tell you: I never seen him look at a woman like he looks at you. I'm not sure how much that means, whether it will get him over that hump he has to cross over to have a real closeness with a woman. I hope you're the one that can reach him, because I think you'd be the best thing that ever happened to him. Just try not to get bushwhacked by it. You're too nice a girl.'

Sarah hadn't expected that long summary, and sat there letting it sink in. Nobody knew O'Brien like Smith, and she valued any observations he might offer her.

'Thanks, Smitty,' she said softly. 'You're a good friend. But I don't want you to worry about me. I've pretty much decided that O'Brien won't ever welcome anybody into his private life, man or woman, on a permanent basis.'

'I hope you're wrong,' he said. 'In my opinion, he'd be crazy to turn his back on a woman like you. But I have to be honest with you. I don't think he'll be in Fort Revenge long. It's the call of the coyote moon.'

'He told me about it,' she said pensively. 'I think he feels it every day. Every night. I can't compete with that.'

Smith sighed. 'Well. He'll be dusting in here in a coupla hours. I reckon he'll be hungry as a winter-starved grizzly. I better make ready for them.'

Sarah rose. 'Thanks for talking with me, Smitty. You're the only one here who knows him.'

'You can come in and decorate this place any time you please,' Smith grinned at her.

★   ★   ★

In the small town of Sulphur Creek in southwest Kansas, Ezra Logan and his grandson rode slowly, walking their mounts so they could look the place over. They were tired and dusty from the long trail.

'I thought it would be bigger than this,' Ezra commented. 'I never thought much of Kansas.'

'Bunch of backwoods cow towns,' Matt said. 'Except for Wichita and Dodge.'

They passed the Sagebrush Hotel and approached a saloon called the Prairie Schooner. 'Is that it?' Matt asked. 'The one Uncle Hank owned?'

Ezra shook his head. 'It's that one farther down the street. The Lost Dogie. Some character named Jennings is running it. He sent the wire about Hank.'

A couple of minutes later they stopped at the Lost Dogie, tethered their mounts, and went in. It was a clean, well-kept saloon, with a nude painting behind the bar and sawdust on the wood plank floor. A middle-aged, round-faced bartender had just served two cowpokes at a nearby table, and was returning to the bar.

'Come on in, boys. What'll you have today?'

'Make it two whiskeys,' Ezra told him. He and Matt sidled up to the bar.

The barkeep served the drinks. 'I guess you boys are new in town?'

Ezra gulped the whiskey. 'Are you Jennings?'

The bartender grinned. 'The same. Barkeep. Owner. Handyman. How's the whiskey, boys?'

Ezra wasn't smiling. 'I'm Ezra Logan. Hank's uncle. This here is my grandson Matt.'

Jennings' face sobered. 'Well, I'll be damned.'

'Bet you figured you'd never set eyes on us.'

Jennings gave a nervous laugh. 'Why, I'm real pleasured to meet you both. Glad you got the wire. Listen, anything I can do for you while you're here in town, just holler. That whiskey is on the house.'

Ezra gave him a sour look. 'So you worked for Hank?'

'Oh, no. That was my older brother. He was killed in a shoot-out here. He had wrote that telegram and forgot to send it. I went ahead and sent it to you after his death.'

'How come you're running the saloon?' Ezra said pointedly.

Jennings now looked a bit worried. 'Why, Luke Mallory, the owner of the Prairie Schooner, inherited it. He's selling it to me.'

Ezra set his glass down. 'This saloon should've gone to the next of kin,' he said deliberately. 'That's me.'

Jennings swallowed hard. 'Well, I don't know. I got papers.'

Ezra grunted. 'We'll want to see them. Later on. In the meantime, what about this snail-slime they call O'Brien?'

'Oh, yes. He was here. Hank went after him, like you wanted. But he shot a boy instead and O'Brien killed him. That's all I know.'

'This O'Brien, what does he look

like?' Matt asked.

Ezra gave him a sober look as Jennings responded. 'Oh, let's see. I only seen him twice. Wears rawhides belted at the waist. Don't carry iron, except for that rifle he's never without. Pretty big guy. Eyes that bore right through a man to the back of his head. Unsettling. An ornery bastard, I hear. You won't get two civil words out of him. Lived out on the trail too long. Half-savage, you know what I mean? That's about it.'

Matt was staring somberly at him, reflecting on that summary. Ezra just grunted out his disdain. 'Do you know where he went from here? We heard he was heading for Indian Territory.'

Jennings shrugged. 'I can't tell you. Ask Marshal Tate down at the jail. Him and that Sumner boy was tight with the hunter. Tate might know.'

Ezra nodded. 'We'll be coming back through here some day soon. Don't forget we're going to have us a talk about the Lost Dogie.'

Jennings' face sobered down again. 'I

don't want no trouble, mister. That's all legal between me and Mallory. You can ask the mayor.'

Ezra didn't respond. He and his grandson quietly left the place and rode on down the street to its south end where the city marshal's office and jail were located. It was just a small whitewashed building with a sign on its front that announced CITY MARSHAL.

When the two riders went inside, they found Uriah Tate sitting behind a weathered old desk, sorting through Wanted dodgers. He looked up at them curiously. He was middle-aged and pot-bellied and did not look the part of a lawman.

'Gentlemen. Can I help you?'

Ezra looked him over arrogantly. He had put better-looking lawmen than this in their graves up in Montana. 'You the law here?'

Tate sat back on his chair. 'That's right.'

'We understand a man named O'Brien came through here not long ago.'

Tate smiled, and nodded. 'Helped us rid this town of gunfighters. Never met a man I liked more.'

As Ezra scowled at that comment, a young man still in his teens came up from the jail cells. He was Jock Sumner, a ward of Tate and a newly appointed deputy. But his duties were mostly clean-up work at the jail. He looked curiously at the two Logans.

'Morning, boys. Nice day out there.'

Matt glanced at Ezra. 'The boy Hank shot.'

Ezra turned on him angrily. 'Shut up, damn it!'

But both Jock and Tate heard him. 'You knew Hank Logan?' Tate said, a new tone in his voice.

Ezra put on a fake grin. 'Don't mind the boy here. We just heard stuff around town.' He wasn't going to admit their identity to Tate yet. 'We're a couple of trappers looking for O'Brien. We hear he rode down into the Territory. Maybe Fort Revenge. We have a mutual friend down there.'

Jock eyed them narrowly. 'What friend would you be talking about?'

Ezra hurled a hot look at Jock. 'We was talking to the marshal here, boy.'

'What's O'Brien's friend's name?' Tate echoed Jock. 'It's a simple question, stranger.'

Ezra tried to keep his cool. 'I don't remember the name off-hand. But I think he runs a stage line down there.'

Tate played it cool, too. 'Yes, I think I recall O'Brien mentioning that. But he didn't head down that direction.'

Ezra frowned heavily. 'That's funny. Our information was pretty definite he rode down there.'

'To Fort Revenge,' Matt said.

Tate rose. 'No, no. He told us he was riding to Texas. Heard there was good trapping down by the Brazos. Was stopping to pick up another man to ride with him. No, it was Texas, boys. You'd have to look there if you want to find him.'

Suddenly Ezra drew the heavy Tranter .38 on his hip, aiming it at

Tate's belly. 'You're a goddamn liar, Marshal.'

Matt drew his Iver-Johnson, too, holding it on Jock.

'You're Logans!' Jock blurted out.

'That's right, boy. Come to make some more Logan history. I ought to plug you both for trying to derail us. But you ain't worth it. You told me what I wanted to know, anyway. We'll find that murdering snake down at Fort Revenge. And we'll make that pile of cow dung wish he never heard of a Logan.'

'O'Brien never murdered anyone in his life,' Jock said emotionally, wondering whether to go for the revolver at his side to save O'Brien's life. Tate saw his look and shook his head at him.

'You want me to finish the job Hank bungled, boy?' Matt hissed out at Jock.

'Don't do anything you'll regret later, boys,' Tate said carefully. 'You ain't in any trouble yet here in Kansas.'

Ezra grinned. 'You're lucky I'm in a good mood today, Marshal. Up north I'd go out of my way to get myself a lawman. We'll be back through here, anyway. We'll probably meet up again.'

'Not if you find O'Brien,' Jock said meaningfully.

'Let me put one in his belly,' Matt pleaded with Ezra.

'Come on, boy. We got other fish to fry.'

They didn't holster their guns until they had left. Tate and Jock listened as they rode off to the south.

'Should we go after them?' Jock said.

Tate shook his head. 'We ain't got the gunpower, boy.'

'I could ride south. To warn O'Brien.'

'You probably couldn't beat them there. And I wouldn't let you. No. We'll have to let it play out.'

'They'll murder O'Brien!' Jock objected. 'They'll back-shoot him, Uriah! That's the kind they are. What can we do?'

'The telegraph line is down from here to the Territory. I doubt it will be back up in time to give any warning. I reckon, as usual, O'Brien is on his own.'

Jock just sat down heavily on to a nearby chair, and stared at his hands. It looked like he was about to lose one of the few real friends he had ever made in his young life.

* * *

It was early evening in Fort Revenge, and O'Brien was rested up from the day. He had returned from Tulsa, volunteered to accompany the stage on another run north to deliver a payroll to a rancher there, then finished off the afternoon on his return by carrying freight boxes from the front porch of the depot to the rear for temporary storage. It was a day that would have put Funk or Bailey in bed for a week. But a meal at the café with Smith had rejuvenated the hunter completely. He hadn't spoken about his encounter in Tulsa. Not long after their supper, O'Brien sat down with Smith in the office.

'I run into a couple of Provost's

men,' O'Brien began.

Smith cast a curious look at him. 'Why the hell didn't you tell me?'

'I am telling you.'

Smith sighed. His boots were up on his desk. 'I never seen such a closed-mouth bastard in all my born days. Go on.'

O'Brien gave him an acid look. 'Like I was saying. I went into a saloon there in Tulsa, and two of them was in there. Some little ferret wearing a Starr .44 and a Bowie come over to me. Pointed out another boy across the room that works for Provost, too. Latham, I think he said. Is he the one that was bothering Sarah?'

Smith liked it that he had asked the question. 'I think so, yes.'

O'Brien made a mental note. 'Anyway, this skinny one with the Bowie wanted to talk about selling the Express.'

'What did you say?'

'What do you think? But they're coming back. No doubt about it. They got their eye on the Express for sure.

They'll put a few dollars on the table, and want our signatures on a bill of sale. They'll figure on using guns to get our names on the paper.'

'They can fry in Hell first,' Smith said belligerently.

'Can you really use that Joslyn you still carry around like Annie Oakley?' O'Brien asked with a narrow smile.

'I can carry my load. Anyway, Annie can shoot almost as good as you, partner. I seen her at a show once.'

'Can she do it with a herd of a thousand buffs trying to knock her horse down so they can trample her to a pulp?' The smile widened slightly.

Smith returned it, staring across the room, reminiscing. 'I doubt it.'

'Can we depend on Reece? If it comes to it?'

Smith nodded. 'He practices with his Smith & Wesson. I think he'd stand with us.'

'Don't even ask Funk or the others. They'd be worthless, and they'd get themselves killed.'

Smith glanced over at him. 'Our good mayor is running scared. He talked to a couple of drifters at Thatcher's saloon this morning.'

O'Brien frowned. 'For recruitment?'

Smith nodded.

'I'll be damned.'

'I know. These boys looked like they could use the guns they wore. Spencer offered them money, and they accepted — till they found out they'd be going up against Frank Provost and his boys. Then they give Spencer his money back and turned tail. They're probably in Kansas by now.'

'You tell him, Smitty, you hire gunfighters for defense, you can end up as bad off as with Provost. That damn saloon should be closed down, then we wouldn't be getting people like that in here.'

'Spencer says it helps the town economy,' Smith said. 'He says we need it to do business with the outside world. Like Dodge City. They got a whole street of saloons.'

'And they had to bring in that gun-fighter Earp to keep the town liveable,' O'Brien said quietly. 'And if it stays clean, it will grow into a Kansas City. Or a Tulsa.'

Smith caught O'Brien's somber look. 'I hear you, partner. But Spencer says it's inevitable. All these little towns will grow. Folks will swarm in here from the East.'

'And the West will be the East,' O'Brien said pensively.

A thought occurred to Smith. 'Is that why you turn your back on that girl? Because she's from Boston? Because you see her as the first of many? Folks who will take your world away?'

O'Brien looked over at him with a stony face. 'What girl?'

Smith knew that he knew what girl. 'There ain't one in a thousand Easterners that could last through what she did with you, partner. Out there on that long trail from Kansas. In hardship camp. Almost getting kidnapped by redskins. All them life-or-death escapades, and nary a complaint from her. She's special, O'Brien. She's very special.'

When O'Brien turned to him, his blue eyes burned into Smith's head. 'You ever mention me and that woman again, you'll have to get yourself a new partner.'

Smith held that frightening look. 'I thought I was a friend. Friends can discuss things.'

'Not this, Smitty. Not ever.' He got up from a straight chair, and left the room.

Smith sighed heavily. Then he called after him.

'Reece is back there somewhere! Send him up here and I'll check out that Smith & Wesson for him!'

6

Frank Provost and his men arrived back in town the following morning, on a rainy, blustery day. They were all out of sorts because of the long ride in the weather, and Provost was long-faced as he looked the main street over for the second time. 'Maybe this place is not worth the effort after all.'

His best man, Skinner, reined up close to him. He moved in his saddle and it squeaked under his weight. 'Yes, it is, Frank. It can be a gold mine for us. Look. They even opened up that saloon down the street.'

Slim Latham, the ladies' man, got a bright look on his face for the first time that day. 'Well, look at that! They plumb civilized this place!'

'Good,' Icepick Munro spat out. 'I need a drink. Bad.'

A few minutes later they all entered

Thatcher's new Stage Trail Saloon. Thatcher was tending bar because his hired man wasn't full-time yet. The Provost gang took a table near the bar as Provost shook rain off his hat. Then Provost turned to a lone customer sitting nearby, a young ranch hand.

'Finish that drink and get out,' Provost said to him curtly. Thatcher was at the far end of the bar and didn't hear the remark.

The cowpoke frowned. 'Who the hell are you?'

'He's the new owner,' Skinner said in a hard voice. 'Frank Provost.'

A changed look. 'Frank Provost?'

'The same,' Icepick grinned.

The cowboy gulped the rest of his drink, got up, and tipped his hat to Provost. 'No problem, boys. I was done, anyway.'

Thatcher came down to the near end of the bar. 'Hey, Wilkins. You had enough already?'

'I'm — due back at the ranch,' was the tense reply. He hurried out.

Thatcher recognized Provost for the first time. 'Oh. You boys are back.'

'We're here to stay,' Latham grinned.

'I guess you've took on another business since we were here,' Provost said. Thatcher was already getting nervous. 'Yes. I thought the town needed a saloon. What can I get you, boys?'

'Bring us a bottle of your best whiskey,' Icepick spoke up.

'Not yet,' Provost corrected him. 'What's your name?' he addressed Thatcher again.

'Ben Thatcher. At your service, boys.'

'Draw up a chair and sit down,' Provost told him.

Thatcher frowned slightly, but got the chair. He set it down beside Provost. 'What can I do for you, Mr Provost? That was your name, wasn't it?'

'I've changed my mind about buying your restaurant,' Provost said.

'Well. Good. It wasn't for sale.'

'You making any money here at the saloon?'

Thatcher shrugged. 'Not much. Nobody knows it's here yet.'

Provost reached into a belt pouch and drew out some paper money. He placed it on the table near Thatcher. 'There's two hundred dollars. I'm buying the Stage Trail.'

Thatcher stared at the wad of money. 'I don't think you boys understand: neither of my businesses is for sale. I expect to run this into a real profitable investment.'

'You don't have the expertise. Skinner here tended bar in Fort Griffin for quite a while. We can make this place hum with business.' He looked around the room. 'You've done nothing with this yet. You got to spend money to make money. The town needs a nice saloon and you can't give it to them.'

'Well, I'd like to try my hand at it, anyway,'Thatcher said quietly. 'I got ideas.'

'That boat has sailed, my boy,' Provost grinned at him. 'Pick that money up and count it.'

Thatcher hesitated, then took the money and counted it out.

'Is it all there?'

'Yes, but — '

Provost pulled a paper from his shirt pocket, and unfolded it. 'I got this bill of sale here. Just put your name on that line marked with an X, and our business will be finished.'

Thatcher stared at the paper.

'It's all legal-like,' Provost assured him. 'Once you sign it, the saloon is mine.'

Thatcher continued to stare at the paper.

'Sign it, stupid,' Skinner growled. 'You're lucky he offered you anything.'

'It's a good deal,' Icepick interjected. 'You can rest easy on that score.'

'Shut up, Icepick,' Provost said nicely.

'First of all, the saloon is worth a lot more than this,' Thatcher argued, stalling for time until he could assess the situation.

'It will be some day,' Provost said. 'But not now.' He looked into Thatcher's eyes. 'You've got no choice in this, Thatcher,' he said slowly.

Thatcher swallowed hard, looking around the table at those hard faces. He wasn't up to standing up to men like these. He didn't think anybody in Fort Revenge was, either. Provost proffered a pencil, and Thatcher took it.

'Can I keep an interest in it?'

'Just sign the damn paper,' Skinner barked at him.

Thatcher scrawled his name on the bill of sale. Provost picked it up, took a quick look at it and returned it to his pocket. Thatcher took the money lying on the table. 'Good,' Provost grinned. 'Now you're sitting with the new owner of the Stage Trail Saloon. Bring us that bottle of whiskey now, Thatcher. We feel like celebrating our first buy in Fort Revenge!'

'And drinks are on the house!' Latham laughed.

Thatcher rose to leave the table, looking tense and bewildered.

'After you get the drinks,' Provost stopped him, 'I'd like you to do me a personal favor.'

Thatcher turned to him, still looking stunned.

'Go get the mayor for me. That boy we met at the café that night. I want to buy him a drink and have a little talk with him.'

Thatcher delivered the whiskey and then left for Mayor Spencer's office. The mayor was at home, which was also the informal city hall. He was in the office, which had been a library in the old Victorian house. Sarah and Abigail Pritchard were both there at small desks, working on the books. Spencer was leaning over Abigail's desk when Thatcher came in, face flushed.

'They're back,' he announced to the room.

They all looked over at him. 'Who's back?' Abigail asked.

But Spencer and Sarah knew.

'They just forced me to sell the saloon.'

Spencer frowned at him hard. 'You sold Provost the saloon?'

'He paid for it. They made it clear I didn't have a choice. What would you have done?'

'You should have said no. And come to us,' Sarah said. 'O'Brien and Smith would want to know.'

'What could they do?' Thatcher argued. 'They'll offer to buy the Express next. They're gunfighters, Mayor. And they don't take no for an answer.'

'You were foolish to do it without talking with the rest of us,' Spencer told him. 'Now they have a foothold here in Fort Revenge.'

'Provost wants to see you,' Thatcher told him.

Spencer frowned again. 'When?'

Thatcher shrugged. 'Now. They're at the saloon. Drinking.'

'Oh, for God's sake,' Spencer muttered.

'Don't go,' Sarah said, standing up. 'These men are dangerous. I'm going down to the depot to tell O'Brien.'

'No, no,' Spencer told her. 'I want to avoid trouble with these men if we can. Let me go over there and see what they've got to say. Maybe they'll be content now that they've got the saloon.'

He gave Thatcher a sheepish look. 'I think we owe it to ourselves and them to let them talk.'

'They'll see your acquiescence as weakness,' Sarah said. 'That's the way they think. It can't hurt to tell O'Brien and Smith what's going on.'

'Just wait till I get back, Sarah. That's all I ask. Please.'

Sarah sighed. 'All right, Mayor. But hurry back. We'll be waiting.'

'We'll be waiting,' Abigail echoed unnecessarily.

'I'll be here with them,' Thatcher told him.

★ ★ ★

When Spencer arrived over at the Stage Trail Saloon, Ira Skinner was behind the bar, picking out another bottle of liquor for the four. They all turned to him when he walked in.

Spencer tipped his hat. 'Mr Provost. Boys. Thatcher tells me you wanted to see me.'

'Well. Our second meeting, Mayor. Why don't you settle yourself on this chair and wet your whistle? We just bought us a goddamn saloon!'

Spencer nodded and seated himself on the chair near Provost. 'That's what I just heard. But I'll pass on the drink.' He removed his hat and ran a hand through silvered hair. He looked tired. And scared.

'We thought we should go right to the top,' Provost smiled at him.

'Right to the top,' Icepick repeated, swigging a drink down.

Ira Skinner returned to his seat at the table, and uncorked the second bottle. This one was rum. 'How long you been mayor here, Spencer?' he said without looking at the mayor.

'Why, I guess it's running on to a decade and a half,' Spencer answered.

'So, I reckon you go back past the Express company, and maybe the café?' Provost pursued.

Spencer nodded, trying to appear calm to them. 'Shanghai Smith started up his company after I'd been here a while. We were all glad to see him come in and put our little town on the map.'

'When did the hunter join him?' Skinner asked pointedly.

'Oh, he just arrived here recently. I think he pumped some much-needed capital into the company.'

'Then the Express wasn't really doing that well?' Provost said very slowly.

'Well . . . ' Spencer started. But could think of nothing to deny it.

'Look, Mr Mayor,' Provost continued. 'I suppose you're looking forward to the day when this little town of yours grows into something you can be proud of. Am I right?'

'Well, of course,' Spencer said, frowning slightly.

'So if somebody came along and wanted to invest big-time in your town that would be a good thing, wouldn't it?'

Spencer was feeling uncomfortable. 'I suppose it would.'

'Well, we're that somebody,' Provost

said. 'We can turn this saloon into a real money-maker. People will come from miles around to drink here. Ranchers. Farmers. Thirsty trail men. Passengers off the stage.'

'Sounds like you have big plans,' Spencer said quietly.

'We can do the same with the Territorial Express,' Provost went on. 'Start up new routes. Put on additional coaches. Make it the center of everything here. Make the town buzz with activity. Activity that would make this little berg rich, Mayor. You'd like that, wouldn't you?'

'Who wouldn't want prosperity?' Spencer said uncertainly.

'The only thing standing in the way of that is the present ownership of the stage line,' Provost concluded slowly.

'Just them two buffalo men trying to run a business,' Icepick put in.

'Shut up, Icepick,' Provost grated out.

Skinner gave Icepick a hostile look, and Slim Latham chuckled softly.

'What are you saying?' Spencer finally answered. 'I don't think either Smith or

O'Brien are of a mind to sell the Express.'

'That's where you come in, Mayor,' Provost told him. 'I'm going to make them a very attractive offer. But if you talk to them first, tell them how they can help Fort Revenge by selling to us, they'll probably change their minds.'

'Oh, I doubt that,' Spencer said, dry-mouthed.

'But you will help us, won't you?' Provost said in a new, hard voice. 'You will tell them how it will be best for you, the town and definitely for them, if they'll be reasonable about this?'

Spencer swallowed back his fear. 'Sure. I'll talk to them.'

Provost clapped him on the back. 'I knew we could count on you.' He looked into Spencer's eyes. 'The wellbeing of this town depends on it.'

'I understand,' Spencer said, a little breathlessly.

And we'd like to see them this evening. Here, at our saloon.'

'I'll tell them,' Spencer said, rising. Then he walked out, head down, his mind spinning with thoughts they had placed there.

★　★　★

Smith and O'Brien were cleaning shot-guns in the long bunk room at the rear of the depot when Spencer came in, panting and red-faced from his quick trip down the street. He had stopped briefly at his house to advise the women and Thatcher what was taking place. Outside it was getting dark, and the Express owners had just returned from the café where they were served by a recent hireling of Thatcher. They knew nothing of the presence of Provost. When Spencer came hurrying in, Smith looked up at him curiously. O'Brien was running a cloth through a gun barrel.

'Provost is back,' Spencer gasped out. 'He wants to see you two.'

O'Brien looked up at him. 'Where are they now?'

'They're at the saloon. They own it now.'

Smith scowled at him. 'Would you try to make sense, Mayor?'

'I'm telling you the truth,' Spencer continued. 'Thatcher sold the Stage Trail. Provost owns it now. He wants to see you there tonight. To buy the Express.'

O'Brien shook his head. 'That boy must have catclaw for brains. I told them two in Tulsa we ain't selling.'

'I don't think they're listening, O'Brien,' Spencer said dully. 'I don't think they're listening to anybody. They tried to convince me the town would be better off with them running the Express.' He glanced over at Smith.

Smith was frowning heavily. 'What did you say then?'

Spencer sighed. 'I didn't say anything. Hell, I was at a table with four fast guns, boys. Don't expect too much of me. I'm not cut out for this sort of thing.' He had sat down on a bunk beside Smith. 'I told them I didn't think you'd sell.'

O'Brien was shaking his head again.

150

'We'll have to go down there.'

'Let's not have any bloodshed, boys. We have a nice peaceful town here. Let's keep it that way.'

O'Brien gave him a stony look which made Spencer's mouth go dry again. 'Go get Reece. We ought to have three guns.'

Spencer looked from him to Smith. 'Guns?'

'They have four, Mayor,' Smith reminded him.

'You can't cause trouble for four gunslingers!' Spencer protested.

'So you'd advise us to just sign over the Express to them?' Smith said, with heavy sarcasm.

'I didn't mean that. Maybe there's some compromise we could reach.'

'We?' O'Brien growled.

'You know. Let them make an investment in the company. But you still control it. Something like that.'

'Did you say anything like that to them?' O'Brien said ominously.

'No, no. I wouldn't do that. But this

151

town doesn't need any big trouble.'

'We're not making it,' O'Brien said flatly. 'Now go find Reece.'

Spencer rose looking very distraught. 'Sure. Reece.'

O'Brien stood, too. 'Where's Sarah?'

'Oh, she was on her way back to Mrs Barstow's. With Abigail.'

'Good. Now you go on home after you get Reece. Keep out of the way.'

Spencer gave him a somber look, and nodded. 'Yes. I'll be at home.'

It was just about an hour later when Ed Reece met Smith and O'Brien outside the saloon. Reece had strapped on his Smith & Wesson and looked very scared. 'Do you think there'll be shooting?' he asked nervously.

O'Brien went over to him and slid the sidearm in and out of its holster.

'Don't you ever oil that thing?'

'I don't ever use it,' Reece admitted.

'Well, let's get in there and make our minds known,' Smith said.

When they got inside, Provost was sitting alone at the same table; Icepick and Skinner were at the bar. Latham was nowhere in sight.

'Well, well,' Provost greeted them. 'The entire company management. Good to meet you, boys.'

Smith and O'Brien walked over to his table, and Reece went over and leaned on the bar, Skinner and Icepick eyeing him with obvious disrespect.

'I'm Smith, and this is O'Brien,' Smith announced to them.

Provost took a moment to look O'Brien over carefully. 'I've heard about you, O'Brien.'

O'Brien was carrying the Winchester loosely, at arm's length. He didn't respond. He was assessing Provost's hardware and that of his men.

'O'Brien is from the north country,' Smith answered for him. 'He ain't much known hereabouts.'

'Well, I guess his reputation precedes him,' Provost offered. 'Take a load off, boys. I'd like to talk some business.'

Smith took a chair and O'Brien followed reluctantly. 'I thought I made all that clear in Tulsa.' He laid the rifle on the table between them. 'The Express ain't for sale.'

Provost glanced soberly at the Winchester. He had already noted that O'Brien wasn't carrying a sidearm. 'Well, now that's exactly why we wanted to talk some more about this. It don't hurt to talk, does it?'

'Get your talking done,' O'Brien told him. 'We got real work to do back at the depot.'

Provost studied that square-jawed, bearded face. He had known that it would be O'Brien who would give them the most trouble.

'We won't waste your time, O'Brien,' Provost said. 'I can promise you that this meeting is very important to you. Very important.'

'So far, it only seems important to you,' Smith said.

Provost sat back on his chair. 'Look, we didn't come here to make trouble. But you boys aren't stage-line owners by trade. You're into something over

154

your heads. We can take your company and make it into something. Put this town on the map. Something you'll never be able to do. I'm giving you a great opportunity here. To get out from under something you're not suited for and get back to hunting, or whatever you want. And we'll pay you five hundred dollars hard cash for the company. You'd never get a better offer.'

'Mister, do you have trouble hearing plain talk?' O'Brien said, the icy glare boring into Provost's head. 'The Express ain't for sale. It won't be for sale tomorrow and it won't ever be for sale. Does that make it clear enough?'

Provost's face clouded over during that summary. Icepick and Skinner exchanged a dark look over at the bar.

'You say your mind pretty heavy, hunter. I came here with courtesy, thinking I was dealing with civilized men. I see I was wrong.'

'Think like you want,' O'Brien said curtly. He grabbed the rifle and rose.

Provost turned to Smith. 'Does this

boy speak for you, or have you got a mind of your own?'

Smith got up, too. 'I think he said it pretty well.' He smiled at Provost. 'The Express is worth several times what you offered, mister. But if you offered ten thousand, we wouldn't sell. We like running the Express. If you want a stage company, start your own. We don't mind a little competition.'

Provost nodded. 'Well, I reckon we'll just have to work on changing your minds. My boys can be very persuasive when they have to be.'

O'Brien cast another cold look on him. 'Mister, you're commencing to get right under my skin.'

Provost rose slowly, his right hand out over the Colt at his side. But Smith laid a hand on O'Brien's arm. 'Come on, partner. I think we wore out our welcome here.'

O'Brien gave Provost a last hard look, then started to turn, noticing for the first time that Slim Latham wasn't present. He remembered that Latham was the one who had harassed Sarah on the gang's first visit. He turned to Smith. 'We're short one smart-ass here.'

Smith nodded. 'Where's your fourth man? Out stealing candy canes from babies?'

Provost just gave him an acid look, but Icepick, over at the bar, responded. 'I think he went out looking for that girl he took a fancy to last time. Wanted to have hisself an entertaining night.' A low laugh.

'Sonofabitch,' O'Brien muttered. He turned to Smith. 'See you back at the depot later.'

Smith nodded, and O'Brien was gone.

'Come on, Reece. We got to get you back home,' Smith said then.

When they were gone, Ira Skinner hauled off and slapped Icepick hard across the face. Icepick drew on him, his lip bleeding. But Provost put an end to it.

'Put that away, Munro, or I'll put one in your left eye.'

A couple moments later they were all drinking again.

O'Brien had arrived at the Victorian boarding-house down the street, but when he reached Sarah's room she wasn't there. He found Abigail Pritchard in the downstairs parlor on his way back out.

'O'Brien! Are you looking for Sarah?'

He nodded. 'Yes. Where is she?'

'Why, she heard that those men are back in town and went down to the depot to make sure you and Smith knew.'

'When did she leave?'

'Quite a while ago. Just before that man came looking for her.'

O'Brien frowned. 'What man?'

She shrugged. 'Said he had city business with her.'

'Hell. Did you tell him where she went?'

She grew a scared look. 'Why, yes. Oh, dear. He wasn't one of them?'

But O'Brien was already out the door. Spencer would be at home now and he knew Smith was heading to Reece's place before he returned to the depot. Sarah would be there alone.

When he arrived at the depot, everything looked normal at first, but then he heard a muffled scream from the bunk room at the rear.

'Goddamn it!' he growled, as he rushed there.

When he got there, Sarah was lying on a bunk with Latham standing over her. Her blouse was torn down the front, and her cheek was red where he had hit her. Tears were running down her cheeks, and she was breathing hard.

Latham was standing over her with a hard grin, unbuckling his gunbelt in preparation to raping her.

'You just be quiet, little lady, and I won't hurt you bad.'

Sarah saw O'Brien first and her eyes widened slightly. Latham saw the reaction and whirled around quickly. He still held the gunbelt, and drew the Schofield .45 from its holster in one swift movement, without speaking, aiming the gun at O'Brien's heart.

But O'Brien had raised the muzzle of the Winchester, and the two guns roared into action at the same moment. Latham's shot creased O'Brien's left shoulder, ripping at his rawhides, and then the fiery hot lead from the rifle struck Latham just below his broken nose, traveled through his brain pan like a hot poker and exploded out the back of his head, spattering matter and blood all over the wall behind him.

Latham ran against the wall, hung there with his limbs jerking for a moment, then slid lifeless to the floor, leaving a crimson stain down the wall.

The room was thick with the pungent odor of gun-smoke.

'Oh, God!' Sarah cried. 'Oh, God!' Tears were streaming down her face.

O'Brien threw the rifle on to a nearby bunk and reached down and picked her up bodily, and let her cry in his arms. They stood there like that for a long moment, then she looked into his eyes. 'I knew you'd come. I knew it.'

'OK. Take it easy now. It's all over. Can you walk?'

She nodded. 'Oh! You're hit!'

'It's a scratch. Let's go up front. Away from this.'

They went and sat together on one of the benches for waiting passengers, and Sarah slowly stopped trembling. She leaned her head on his big shoulder, and he let her.

'You showed a lot of grit back there.'

'He was going to — '

'I know. And he might not let you live to talk about it, neither.'

She raised her head and looked at him, and he thought she had never looked prettier. Maybe because of what had just happened, he had strong urges toward her that he had to push back down, and of which he was slightly ashamed.

'You know, I'd be dead more than once if you hadn't been there.'

He didn't know what to say. 'Things can work out OK sometimes when you're sure they won't.'

She dried her eyes, then impulsively reached over and kissed him on his cheek. O'Brien was surprised. He caught her gaze, frowning, trying even harder to push that incredibly intense emotion away before it engulfed him.

She saw the frown. 'I'm sorry. I shouldn't have done that.'

His mouth had gone dry. 'It's OK, Sarah. Look, I'd better get you home. We'll have the local vet look at you. You might need a pill.'

'No,' she said, shaking her head. 'I just want rest.'

He found his breath was coming just a trifle fast, and it disturbed him. 'I'll get my rifle. Smitty and me will clean up back there later. But now, I'll get you on home.'

A few minutes later they stepped out into the blackness of the much-too-eventful night.

7

'What did you say?' Frank Provost replied, in an iron-hard voice to Icepick. He was sitting on the edge of a cot in a back room of the saloon, pulling on his boots. The four gunmen had brought in cots, to sleep, at least temporarily at the Stage Trail. Ira Skinner, sitting on a nearby cot, frowned toward Icepick.

'I saw it myself,' Icepick said, wild-eyed. He was always up ahead of everybody else because he couldn't sleep more than a few hours at night. 'Latham is down at the morgue with quarters on his eyes!'

Provost had realized Latham wasn't back when they all went to bed, but figured he was staying all night with some woman.

'Latham is dead?' he said in bewilderment, trying to focus on what

Icepick was saying.

'As a doornail,' Icepick said breezily. 'Got a hole in the back of his head you could stuff your fist into.'

Skinner rubbed at his face. 'What the hell happened?'

'The mortician says O'Brien found him with that girl we met the first time here. Latham was having his way with her. The hunter come in, saw what was happening, and blasted Latham into eternity.'

'He murdered him in cold blood?' Provost said, his voice going frigid.

'No, Latham got a shot in. Word is he wounded the hunter.'

Skinner and Provost exchanged a stormy look.

'I knew he would be the one to cause us trouble,' Provost muttered. 'I always knew it would be him. Even before we met him.'

'He just reduced our numbers,' Skinner said. 'He has to be taken care of. He's our only problem here. With him gone, that fat partner of his will fold like a gypsy tent.'

Provost sat there, kneading his hands. 'From this minute on, we focus all of our attention on getting O'Brien. Nothing else matters until he's six feet under.'

Icepick leaned toward Provost. 'Let me have him, Frank. I'll find him tonight and run this through his kidney.' He unsheathed the razor-sharp Bowie and showed it to Provost.

'Put that thing away! He'd take that from you and slice you up into little pieces.'

Icepick's face colored. 'Now wait just a minute.'

'The hunter is smart,' Provost went on, ignoring Icepick's protest. 'And good. He'll have to be brought down with fast guns. That's Skinner and me.'

'What about me?' Icepick glared.

'You too. We'll want all the guns we can muster. We'll try to get him down here for one more talk. Alone. If the big one comes too, he won't be any trouble.'

'They won't talk business again,' Skinner said.

'I know. Maybe we make up a little story. Say we gave up on getting the Express, and want to know if they're interested in buying the saloon back before we offer it to Thatcher. I think they didn't want it open in the first place. We'd ask to see O'Brien specifically.'

'Will they buy that, after Latham?' Icepick suggested.

Provost looked up at him. 'Finally. Using your head. We'll have to tell them that we understand what happened to Latham. I think if we stress that we're returning to Tulsa after our meeting, O'Brien will come. He'll never walk back out of here alive.'

'It's a good plan,' Skinner agreed. 'And if he don't come, we'll go after him.'

'Get him any way we can,' Provost said.

Icepick stood there, though, looking disappointed. Provost had lost respect for him, he figured. And he was the one to take the hunter down. Alone. He would show Provost he was a valuable member of the gang. Provost would need a good man, now that Latham was gone.

Icepick nodded quietly. 'Yeah. Any way we can.'

'We ought to act now,' Skinner suggested.

Provost nodded. 'Icepick, go find Smith. He'll be easier to convince. Then he'll persuade O'Brien. Make it clear we don't give a damn about Latham. You understand?'

Icepick nodded. 'Sure.'

'Be friendly. Apologize for Latham's rude behavior. Tell them we'll be here whenever they can break free. Make it clear we'll be returning to Tulsa. You got all that?'

Icepick nodded again.

'Maybe I better go,' Skinner said.

Icepick turned a fiery look on him. 'Like hell you will!'

'It's all right,' Provost said. 'I think

he's got it. I need you here. To talk.'

'Damn right I've got it,' Icepick said hostilely, remembering Skinner's slap on the face the previous evening.

'All right, all right,' Provost said. 'They might be doing morning chores together. Walk down there after we grab some grub at the café. And do it properly.'

It was early afternoon when Icepick walked down to the depot. Old Scratch was there sitting at Smith's desk, but neither Smith nor O'Brien were anywhere in sight.

'Hey, old-timer. Where's your boss?'

Scratch peered up at him from under a green visor. 'Oh. You're one of them. Why do you want Smith?'

Icepick sighed, impatient already. 'I want to talk, you old turkey. What's it your business?'

Scratch frowned. 'It ain't courtesy to use that saucy line, mister. You're talking to a Territorial Express driver.'

'All right, sweetie. With brown sugar on it. Where's Smith?'

'He's off on the stage this afternoon. Had to report that death last night to the county coroner,' he said with a small, satisfied smile.

Icepick restrained himself, and forgot for the moment that he was supposed to make their invitation to Smith if possible. 'Where's that other one? O'Brien?'

'Oh, him? He's down at the hostler's. Checking on that horse of his. Does it every day. Like clockwork.'

Icepick nodded. 'Much obliged.'

'I wouldn't bother him, though. He seemed right ornery this morning.'

Icepick grunted and stepped outside. He looked toward the hostelry, and got an idea that seemed to take possession of him.

Here was his chance, handed to him on a silver platter. His opportunity to show Provost what he was worth. The hunter would be completely distracted by tending his mount. A sitting duck.

It was too tempting to resist.

His cheeks flushed slightly as he

walked clown the street toward the hostler's. He loosened the Starr .44 in its holster, sliding it in and out several times. He would be a small hero to the rest of them soon. They would see him for what he was.

When he arrived there, he was sweating slightly from the warm sun. The hostler met him at the big doorway. 'I can't do no business now. I'm on my way to the café. I ain't ate all day.'

'It's OK. I was looking for O'Brien.'

'Oh. He's way at the back with that Appaloosa of his. Treats it like it was his wife. You'll find him there. I'll be back later.'

Icepick nodded as the hostler walked off. He felt himself tightening up inside as he carefully walked to the rear of the big stable barn, past horses being boarded there. There was a smell of manure mixed with sawdust. A little ripple of fear and excitement passed through Icepick's body.

Then he saw O'Brien. His back was

to him, and he had his big hand on the horse's muzzle. The Winchester was leaning against the front of the stall near him but just out of reach.

'All right, you overgrown prairie dog. You're welcome.' He had just fed it a carrot from the general store. The horse guffered quietly.

'Yeah. You and me are going to take us a gallop tomorrow. Blow some stink off of you. I know you miss it.'

Icepick was halfway there. His gun was still in its holster. He was afraid to draw it before he could use it, in case the hunter heard it. His riding spurs were off, and he moved noiselessly down the long aisle. A horse in a stall he passed made a brief noise but O'Brien paid no attention.

He was over halfway. Then two-thirds. Just ten yards from O'Brien. He stopped, preparing to draw. Then he head the voice call out from behind him.

'Hey, back there! O'Brien!' It was the hostler, who had retraced his steps toward the café. 'Forgot to tell you! I plan to curry-comb that animal later this afternoon!'

O'Brien turned and saw Icepick standing there. They just stared at each other. Then O'Brien called back, 'Good! He needs it!' And he retrieved the rifle.

The hostler left for good then. Icepick remained facing O'Brien, who was now armed.

Icepick forced a grin on to his sallow face. 'O'Brien.'

'What the hell are you up to?' O'Brien said slowly.

'Why, not a thing. This is just a friendly visit.'

'You don't know friendly,' O'Brien responded. 'How long you been standing there? Couldn't you get up your nerve to do it?'

Icepick's face lost the grin. 'I told you. I'm here to make you a friendly offer. You and Smith.'

'We told you: we don't do business with weasels.'

The tic at the corner of Icepick's mouth jerked a fake smile on to his lower face. But his burning gaze belied that message. 'Ain't you still being a little stiff-necked about all this? I'm trying to tell you we don't want the Express no more.'

O'Brien regarded him narrowly. 'Who says?'

'This is straight from Provost. He sent me here.'

'He sent you here to murder me?'

Icepick relaxed some. 'He sent me here to find out if you want the saloon. Before he sells it back to Thatcher.'

O'Brien narrowed down his blue eyes. 'Why would he sell the saloon when he just bought it?'

Icepick shrugged. 'Because of you. If he can't have the Express, he don't want to invest in the town. We'll be riding back to Tulsa. Provost has some business connections there. Some investment ideas.'

'When you re-sell the Stage Trail, you'll be leaving town?' O'Brien said suspiciously.

'That's right. And never bother you no more. And Provost says all is forgiven about Latham. He was always trouble with women. And you can have the saloon back at the same price we paid for it.'

O'Brien made a sound in his throat. 'This is a very sudden change of plans on his part. It don't seem like him.'

'I think he's tired of all the trouble you give him. He has bigger fish to fry back in Tulsa. He has the idea that if you bought the saloon, you could close it down if you wanted, or run it how you liked. Instead of Thatcher.'

O'Brien thought about that.

'You should present this to Smith. He's the major owner of the Express, aint he?' With heavy emphasis.

O'Brien ignored the question. 'If all that's true, then you come down here on your own, didn't you? Because you thought you could take me in a back-shoot. And then Smith would be easier to persuade. Or maybe Provost never intended to return to Tulsa.

174

Maybe he intended to kill me when he got us over there.'

Icepick's eyes gave it away that O'Brien was right. 'Why, that's just bull pucky, hunter. Did I have my gun out? You'd be dead now if I did.'

O'Brien smiled that rare smile. 'You'd be dead now if you did.'

Icepick was so frustrated that he had to prevent himself from drawing the Starr by force of will. But after all, he should be able to beat the rifle. His hand went out toward the gun just a little.

'Do it,' O'Brien told him. 'You been wanting to ever since Tulsa. Make yourself a big man to Provost.'

Icepick licked dry lips, and relaxed the gunhand. 'I told you. We just want to talk. I suggest you talk it over with your partner. We'll be gone hours after the deal is made.'

O'Brien grunted. 'I'll tell him.'

'Good. That's all we want. Some reasonable talk.'

O'Brien watched him leave then,

shaking his head. 'How did that ugly boy live this long?'

Smith was back at the depot when O'Brien returned from the hostelry and they discussed Provost's offer to meet with them, and Smith thought that it could be a veiled invitation to a show-down. But O'Brien figured they had to do it, and Smith agreed. They intended to go to the saloon the following evening when the driver Reece would be free from runs. They sent that message to Provost through another driver, Cinch Bug Bailey.

After a midday meal at the café, where Thatcher grilled them at length about current developments, with the two not mentioning the saloon sale offer to Thatcher, O'Brien walked over to Mayor Spencer's house where he found Sarah alone at her desk. Spencer was out, and Abigail had returned to the rooming-house for her midday meal.

When O'Brien walked in carrying his rifle, Sarah let a beautiful smile decorate her already-lovely face. Her long hair was down on her shoulders, and she was dressed in a green gingham dress that showed off her full figure. O'Brien just stared at all that before either of them spoke.

'O'Brien! What a nice surprise! Did you want to see the mayor? He's over at the Prairie, eating.'

He sat down on a chair beside her desk, and his over-powering masculine proximity made her all a-flutter inside. She tried unsuccessfully to hide it, but O'Brien didn't notice, anyway. He leaned the rifle against the desk.

'I can't believe you look so — rested. After that ordeal.'

'I started recovering as soon as you entered that room,' she confessed.

'He'll be buried tomorrow. I don't think there will be many mourners.'

'When will they leave, O'Brien?' Nobody ever called him anything but his last name, because nobody knew his Christian name except Smith and Sarah. On their adventurous trail south he had given it to her but asked her never to use it, and she hadn't.

'I think they'll leave when we find a way to make them,' he said. He reached into the wide belt at his waist and withdrew a Harrington .38 pocket pistol. It was half the size of a Colt, and weighed half as much. He turned it over in his thick hand.

'I got this for you. You told me you can shoot.'

She looked somber. He proffered the gun, and she took it gingerly. 'I don't need this. With you here.'

He hated compliments, but not when Sarah offered them. He took a deep breath in. 'I'm not with you all the time. We were very lucky with Latham. I don't even like to think about what could have happened.'

He had never said anything so intimate. He was looking down at his hands, and she wanted to jump up, throw her arms around him, and smother him with affection. But she remembered what Smith had said about scaring a wild animal off by pushing too hard.

'I appreciate that, O'Brien. Very much. I'll take the gun.'

'I want you to carry it in your purse,' he said. 'It won't do you any good if it's in a drawer at Mrs Barstow's. Keep it under your pillow at night.' He thought for a moment. 'I think that's it.'

Her eyes had gone moist through that summary and she had to wipe at one. 'I'll take good care of it,' she promised.

He sat back on the chair. 'Now that you been here a while, Sarah, how do you feel about Fort Revenge? Your job here? Your friends?'

She couldn't tell him that it would all have been just tolerable without him there. 'Why, I've settled in quite nicely, I'd say. I haven't met anybody here that I didn't like.'

He nodded. 'That's good.'

She tilted her head slightly. 'Why do you ask?'

'Oh, I don't know. You was a librarian

in Boston, Sarah. You lived a protected life. I reckon you never had to carry a gun in your purse there.'

She laughed. 'No, I never carried a gun. But we weren't crime free, you know. Billy the Kid came from our area.'

'But he didn't go gun-crazy till he come out here,' O'Brien said. 'Maybe it's the West that makes men act different.'

'You're originally from the Carolinas, aren't you?'

'Growed up in the Shenandoah Valley. Same country Daniel Boone was raised in. Killed my first bear when I was eight. Was trading with local Indians when I was ten. Shot all the meat for the table.'

'Do you still have family there?'

He shook his head. He removed his Stetson and ran fingers through long dark hair. Sarah's pulse rate rose without her knowing it. 'They all was took down in a diphtheria epidemic. My daddy. Ma. Sister.'

He sat there.

'Were you close to your father?'

'He taught me how to shoot. Big man, Highlander Scot. Come over here running from something. Brought his Welsh bride with him. He could get ornery when he was drinking.' He paused, remembering. 'My dog got sick once and he brought a shotgun out to shoot it. I got my rifle and stood between him and the dog, and said if he shot the dog, I'd shoot him.'

Sarah's eyes widened slightly. 'What happened?'

'He laughed so hard he almost fell over. Then he put the shotgun away. My dog lived another five years.'

Sarah felt honored. O'Brien never talked about his past to anybody. 'What if he'd shot the dog?'

O'Brien shrugged. 'I'll never know. But I doubt I'd have done it. I was only fourteen.'

Sarah felt closer to him in that moment than she ever had. She restrained herself from reaching out to touch his hand.

'I must be a hardcase today. I never talk about them things.'

Sarah chose her words carefully. 'It pleased me very much. I know you better now. Who you are.'

He looked irritated with himself.

'My parents died when I was just eighteen. Very much like you. I had to find a way to support myself. I took menial jobs. Then I met this man. We were together for a short time, then I found out he was seeing other women. I think he loved himself more than he ever would me. I left him and eventually found the position at the Boston Public Library. I made a few friends, but nothing lasting. Then I saw the ad for mail-order brides. You pretty much know the rest.'

'So you was kind of drifting. Like me.'

Sarah liked where this was going. 'Why, yes. Like you.' A big, lovely smile.

O'Brien looked at his hands again. 'I been thinking,' he said. 'How this ain't no place for a woman like you.'

Her smile faded. 'Oh, no. I've begun

to like the West. Yes, it's all new and hard at first, but I've decided to make it my home.'

O'Brien looked over at her. 'I think you'd make a better life back in Boston, Sarah.'

Her new feeling of elation about this recent sharing of intimacies faded from her insides, and was replaced by tension. And a mild anger.

'What are you saying? Would it be all right with you if I left Fort Revenge and returned to Boston?' She waited breathlessly for an answer.

He met her look with a steady one. 'What I want for you is a safe, happy life. I don't think you can find that here.'

'I see.' She looked away from him.

'I'm only thinking of your best interests,' he said very quietly.

When she turned to him again, there were tears in her green eyes. 'You told me you were proud of the way I conducted myself on our way here from Kansas.'

'Well, I was. I still am.'

'You said I behaved like a western woman.'

'Sarah — '

She rose from her desk, and turned away from him again. 'I have to check some records. And I'm sure you have work to do at the depot.'

O'Brien stood up, and set the Stetson on his head. He grabbed the Winchester. 'Well. I'll be talking to you later, then.'

'We'll see,' she said stiffly.

He stood there for a brief moment, then left the house.

* * *

O'Brien and Smith were now concentrating all of their thoughts on the following night when they would walk down to the saloon and meet Provost for an alleged talk about selling the place to them. But they both knew what Provost really wanted: he was going to have it out with them. Once and for all.

At suppertime they went to the café for a light meal. Thatcher was serving customers. There were only three others when they arrived, and because the whole town knew what was happening, all eyes were on them as they found a table. When Thatcher saw them, he hurried over and began talking in a low, conspiratorial tone.

'What is this I'm hearing? That you boys are buying the Stage Trail?'

'Oh,' Smith said caustically. 'You found out.'

'Well, I'll be damned! You're planning to steal my saloon away from me? I thought you was my friend, Smith.' He gave O'Brien a hard look.

'Settle down, Thatcher,' O'Brien said easily. 'We ain't buying the saloon.'

'That's Provost's idea,' Smith said in his loud voice. 'He wants to use that to lure us into a show-down. Winner take all.'

Thatcher thought about that for a moment. 'Oh.'

'They've already got the saloon,'

O'Brien reminded him, 'because you sold it to them. You can't be any worse off when this is all over with.'

'So. There's going to be shooting?'

'Only if they want it,' Smith replied for them.

'Good Jesus.'

'We both decided we'd try that stew tonight,' O'Brien told him.

'We never had no shooting in Fort Revenge till you come here,' Thatcher said accusingly, looking at O'Brien. 'No offense, but you're bad luck for this town, hunter.'

Smith reached out and grabbed Thatcher by the shirt front and yanked him violently down to eye level.

'You think O'Brien invited them trail scum to Fort Revenge?' he said, in an angry voice rarely heard in Shanghai Smith.

'Well. No.'

'Then I think you owe this boy an apology.'

O'Brien shook his head. 'Forget it. I wouldn't give a lead nickel for this bird-brain's opinion.'

But Smith was still fiery-eyed. 'I swear, you got more trouble keeping your mouth closed than a netted trout, Thatcher.'

Thatcher didn't look remorseful. 'Sorry if I spoke out of turn, boys. I'll just go fetch that stew for you.'

'Just don't try to do too much thinking on stuff like that,' Smith said, as Thatcher moved away. 'You ain't good at it.'

'He ain't entirely wrong,' O'Brien said, when Thatcher was gone. 'I do seem to attract trouble like a magnet sometimes.'

'It's just that you stand up to trouble,' Smith said. 'Most folks don't, so no fuss is made and it don't seem like trouble.'

O'Brien frowned. 'You could have been a damn lawyer, Smitty.'

Smith looked down at his thick hands. 'That's just it, I been doing some thinking. About us, and the Express.'

O'Brien's frown deepened.

'You're a kind of Johnny-come-lately

in the company,' Smith went on slowly. 'You only rode in here a few weeks ago, chaperoning that lovely little lady you barely talk to now.'

A mild irritation crossed O'Brien's square face. 'Goddamn it, Smitty.'

'No, wait. This ain't about Sarah, it's about you and me.'

'Well, are you going to say it or not?'

'You've already hinted that maybe you ain't cut out for this life. I get it, and that's on me. I kind of talked you into this. This world of counting passengers and keeping books and sometimes riding the stage.'

'Are you ever going to actually say something?' O'Brien wondered.

'What I'm saying is, it wouldn't be any big loss to you if we sold the Express to Provost.'

The frown reappeared on O'Brien's face. 'Have you gone out of your mind, partner?'

'I'm not talking about giving it away like he wants. I mean, getting a decent price for it.'

'For God's sake, you love this company, Smitty. I could see it in your face as soon as I got here. Why would you suddenly want to sell? And to a piece of cow dung like Provost?'

Smith shrugged. 'You wouldn't be facing this showdown if it wasn't for me, O'Brien. You'd be off somewhere in Colorado skinning pelts. And let's face it, it's you they're going after tomorrow. They know if they take you out, I won't be able to stop them. So if they get you, I'll lose the company anyway.'

'They won't get me,' O'Brien said, in that off-hand manner.

'But if that happened,' Smith said quietly, 'after I'd got you into this, well, I couldn't handle it.'

O'Brien took a deep breath in, and caught Smith's eye. 'Smitty, you didn't get me into this, Provost did. And you didn't talk me into nothing. I thought the stage-line idea was a good one. You know you can't talk me into anything if I don't like it.'

Smith tried an awkward grin. 'Well.'

Just at that moment Thatcher returned with their stew. 'Here you are, boys. The best stew in five counties!'

When neither man looked up at him, he stood there for an awkward moment, then turned and disappeared into the kitchen.

8

It was a pitch-black night in the Territory. A long day's ride north of Fort Revenge, in hardship camp alongside a small stream, Ezra Logan and his gunslinger grandson Matt were squatting on their saddles beside a camp-fire that sent bright red sparks up into the darkness.

It was still mid-evening. They had a meal of beef jerky, corn dodgers, and hot coffee boiled over the crackling fire. They sat silent, Ezra nursing a last cup of coffee from a beat-up tin cup. Off in the near distance somewhere a coyote wailed into the night.

'If that critter shows hisself I'll shoot him right between the eyes,' Matt grumbled. He was cold, still a little hungry, and he hated coyotes. He had used them for target practice ever since he was a boy.

'Save your ammo,' Ezra muttered.

'You're going to need it. We must be within a day's ride of Fort Revenge.'

Whenever Ezra mentioned their reason for this trek south, Matt felt a ripple of excitement race through him. It was like going hunting. Except this was for the biggest game of all.

'When we get there, Ezra . . . '

Ezra looked over at him. 'Yeah?'

'Let me have him. Don't I deserve it, after this long ride? You got all this experience behind you. All these things you done. I ain't hardly had a chance to prove myself yet. It would be great to say I took O'Brien down. Folks would know about it. I'd get some respect.'

Ezra threw his coffee grounds into the fire and they sizzled there for a moment. 'If half the stories they tell about that murderer is true, he's dangerous. We let it go down the way it will. I'm not going to miss our chance at him just to give you the credit, boy. It might take both of us, and that's the way we'll approach it. Who gets him, gets him. It's our family honor at stake here. Not who gets bragging rights.'

'Well, I just meant . . . you know.'

'Quit thinking about how it will happen. We can't know that yet. I'll make plans when we get there. When we get the lay of the land.'

Matt started to respond, when Ezra held up his hand. A moment later there was the distinct sound of hoofbeats. A rider was walking his mount toward their camp. They both drew their guns as he appeared in the light of their campfire.

'Easy, boys. I ain't carrying. Saw your fire and hoped you might have a cup of real coffee to share with a tired prospector.'

When they saw he was unarmed, they both reholstered the guns. They looked him over. He was dressed in ragged clothing, and a mule was tethered to his mount, bulging saddle-bags on its irons. Ezra and Matt exchanged a look.

'Come on in, stranger,' Ezra spoke up. 'I think we can afford you a cup of coffee.'

The prospector dismounted, picketed

his mount with a ground stake, and came over to the fire. He was an old man, looking weather-worn from age and the trail. 'Mighty good of you boys,' he said in a gravelly voice as he took a cup of steaming coffee from Matt. 'Glad to run into you. I ain't see'd another human being for almost a month.'

They were all standing now. 'So you say you've been prospecting?' Ezra said to him.

The old fellow nodded. 'I heard a rumor about gold in the buttes hereabouts. Been out here for three months and some.'

Ezra and Matt exchanged a second look.

'So what kind of luck you been having, old-timer?' Matt asked.

'Oh, it's been hard digging. I ain't had no luck at all. And then my dog went and got hisself a tapeworm. I cut some prickly pear for a remedy, but he give it up a couple weeks ago.' He sighed. 'That boy was my only friend.'

Ezra nodded his lack of interest. 'We

could spare some bacon fat in that tin over there for you to wallop in a last corn dodger, if you're hungry.'

The old fellow accepted, and wolfed the corn bread down. While he ate, Matt sidled over and looked closer at the saddle-bags on the mule. 'I reckon what you dug up so far would be in these saddle-bags?'

'Oh, there ain't much in there,' the old fellow said blithely. 'Blankets. Sluice pans and such.'

'What about gold?' Ezra asked carefully.

The prospector looked at him with a new expression on his grizzled face. 'Why, there ain't no gold. I wish there was, boys. But I just didn't have no luck this time out.' He looked from one face to the other, and swallowed the last of the corn muffin.

'Maybe you wouldn't mind us looking in them bags?' Ezra said in a harder voice. 'You could pay us a little for the meal we give you.'

The old man looked scared for the

first time. 'I'd pay you something if I had it, boys. But there ain't nothing in them bags for you.'

'Seems like you're pretty anxious for us not to look,' Matt said slowly.

The prospector stared at their faces again. 'You got it all wrong, boys. You won't get nothing by stealing from me. But I don't want you going through my digging stuff. You understand.'

'How much gold you got in them bags?' Ezra asked flatly.

The old man frowned. 'You got to take my word for it, mister. I'd really give you some if I had it. But I told you: them buttes was all played out.'

Ezra looked over at Matt, and nodded. Matt drew his Iver-Johnson .32 and held it on the prospector.

'Hey! What's going on here, boys?'

'Come on, old fellow,' Matt said. 'Even if you ain't lying about the gold, we can sell them animals and equipment at the next town. Let's take a little walk into that stand of trees over there.'

'On second thought, you can have

anything in them bags,' the prospector said then, thick-tongued.

'Move, old-timer,' Matt told him, nudging him with the revolver.

A moment later they were in the stand of young cotton-woods, and a shot rang out. Then Matt returned to the fire alone. 'He won't be found in there for quite a spell.'

'Well, we're his heirs,' Ezra grinned. 'Let's see what he left us.'

They rummaged through the bags for fifteen minutes, throwing equipment on to the ground more and more angrily. Then they looked through the saddle-bags on the prospector's mount. Finally, Ezra took in a deep breath.

'That old fool was telling the truth. He really didn't have no gold.'

'Goddamn old coot!' Matt grumbled. He went over and kicked the mule in the side, and it guffawed loudly once.

'Sonofabitch!' Ezra complained.

'Well, at least we got the animals,' Matt offered. 'And some pans and such.'

Ezra came over and slapped Matt

hard across the face.

'Jesus! What was that for?'

'That look you give me. You made me think there was gold. Now we got a corpse over there, and just for two animals. Get his shovel off the mule, and bury him.'

'What?'

'You heard me, boy. We don't want nothing to interfere with what we come down here for. Now get it done.'

Matt knew it was dangerous to argue too much with his grandfather. A moment later he was heading into the trees with the prospector's shovel.

★   ★   ★

At about that same time in Fort Revenge, one of the Express stages dusted in to a stop at the depot, and several passengers debarked, locals from town and nearby ranches. There were several passengers who were going on north to a crossroads town and ranches, so R.C. Funk and Ed Reece were continuing on after a brief stop. But when they came into the office to find out if there was any mail to take with them, and to get a quick cup of water, O'Brien spoke to Reece.

'Let Old Scratch take your place on the north run,' he said. 'We'll be wanting to talk with you here.'

'Old Scratch?' Funk complained, standing near Reece. 'He ain't no good at shotgun.'

'He'll drive,' O'Brien told him. 'You'll ride shotgun.'

Reece understood what it was all about, but Funk had no idea. He looked over at Smith, at a second desk. 'Is this something new? Changing drivers in mid-run?'

'Just do what O'Brien says, Funk. He's in charge of drivers' schedules. Scratch is out back. Wake him up.'

Funk left, grumbling about the change, and Reece seated himself beside O'Brien's small, weathered desk, sipping a tin cup of cool water. 'Any trouble at the saloon?'

'Not yet,' Smith answered for them,

looking over at O'Brien. Pulling Reece off the coach had been O'Brien's last-minute idea, and he hadn't had a chance to discuss it, so Smith was just as curious as Reece.

'I reckon this is about Provost, though,' Reece went on.

O'Brien nodded. 'I thought the three of us ought to have us a little talk. And the sooner the better.'

'I'm with you,' Reece said. 'But I heard something about Provost in Tulsa.'

They both regarded him soberly. 'Go on, Ed,' Smith told him.

'Turns out this guy has won awards for his shooting. He never misses. And his draw is fast as greased lightning. He's a dangerous one, boys.'

Smith glanced over at O'Brien, to see his reaction. As far as he could tell, there was none.

'He's wanted for murder as far away as Dakota,' Reece went on. 'And at least a couple of his victims have been lawmen.'

O'Brien was getting bored with the

summary. 'Anything else? Or maybe you're going to tell us how he likes his steaks fried.'

Reece gave him a narrow look. 'I thought maybe this stuff was important to us.'

'Is that all of it?' Smith asked in a genial tone.

'One last thing. That boy named Icepick. They say he's real good with that Bowie he carries on his belt. Seems he's killed with it.' He looked over at O'Brien. 'He was bragging in Tulsa that he's going to cut your heart out with it and have it for supper.'

The room fell silent. Finally, O'Brien spoke again. 'Are you finished now, Reece? We got business to discuss here.'

Reece nodded, looking nettled. 'Sure. Whatever you say.'

O'Brien looked over at Smith. 'I been thinking about this hooraw with Provost. Looks like we're letting him do it all his way.'

Smith frowned. 'Go on, partner.'

'First of all, I went and checked the

gun cabinet today. You got four unused Remington eight-gauges in there, all double-barrel and ready to go. And you got plenty of cartridges. Right?'

'Right,' Smith answered, frowning.

'Then when we meet them, we'll all be carrying shotguns.'

'Shotguns?' Reece responded in surprise.

Smith was thinking about that. He nodded. 'Don't require the same accuracy as a sidearm or rifle in a showdown with revolvers. Will put a man down with one hit. Good for close-up work. I like it. Wyatt Earp used one to kill Curly Bill Brocius.'

'You're really giving up that Winchester of yours?' Reece wondered.

'Going up against three of them, yes.'

'Well, count me out,' Reece said. 'I'm clumsy as a hog on ice with one of them things. It's OK on the stage, but in a close-up saloon fight, I think I'd do much better with my Smith & Wesson.'

O'Brien shrugged. He wasn't counting on Reece for a lot of help, anyway.

'Suit yourself. It's your neck at stake.'

'Good. I'll oil the revolver tomorrow morning.'

'You won't have that long,' O'Brien told him.

Now Reece and Smith were both frowning curiously again. 'What are you saying, O'Brien?' Smith asked. 'We agreed on tomorrow night.'

'We're going tonight,' O'Brien said.

Smith sat back heavily on his chair. Reece gasped.

'Tonight?' Reece said hollowly.

'They're relaxed tonight. Probably drinking hard. They're in a mood to go to bed soon, and sleep it off. Get their heads right for tomorrow. They won't expect us.'

Smith ran a big hand over his beard. 'I got to admit it makes my breath come short. But it could work.'

Reece was suddenly flushed in the face. 'That's right! They'd never expect us! Why don't we just go in blasting? It would all be over in seconds. And with less danger to us!'

O'Brien scowled at him. 'We ain't murderers, Reece. Maybe they'll decide it ain't worth it, and leave for Tulsa. The law can deal with them there.'

Reece was embarrassed. 'Well, I don't want to murder nobody, but if anybody deserved it . . . '

'You just take your cues from me when we get there,' O'Brien told him. 'Even tonight they'll probably want to talk. Let them have their say. Then we'll reject any offer they make and see what happens.'

Now Reece felt a slight quivering inside him. 'When will we be going over there? I got some extra ammo at home.'

'We're going now,' O'Brien said. 'Is your gun loaded?'

Reece nodded uncertainly.

'Then you got enough. Let's go arm ourselves, Smitty.'

As they rose to walk down the hall to the gun cabinet, Funk returned with Old Scratch, who was yawning and scratching himself.

'You see what I got for a driver?'

Funk said acidly. 'Thanks a lot, boys.'

'When you get back, make sure that coach is clean before you leave it,' Smith told him. 'And don't let Old Scratch tipple no whiskey on the way.'

'I don't drink on a run!' the old fellow protested weakly.

'Just get out there and get those passengers safely home. We'll see you when you get back,' Smith said, wondering if that were true.

Smith and O'Brien picked out the two best-looking Remingtons, and loaded them with two cartridges each. Smith then picked up another few to put in his belt.

'Put them back,' O'Brien said.

Smith regarded him quizzically.

'You won't have time for reloading. If you can't do it with what's in there, you might as well say a quick prayer and throw the gun on the floor.'

Smith put the cartridges back and sighed heavily. Up front in the passenger waiting room, Reece was checking the ammo in his Smith & Wesson, a

nervous look on his face. Smith and
O'Brien joined him there. O'Brien had
left his rifle in the company office, since
there was no way to use it this night
now. Smith had removed the Joslyn .44
from his waist, and looked much more
formidable with the shotgun.

'Ready, Reece?' Smith asked him.

Reece slid his revolver in and out of
its holster, and nodded. His mouth was
paper-dry.

'Now remember,' Smith said. 'Let
them have their say. Even if they're
under the weather from booze.'

'If they offer to return to Tulsa,'
O'Brien said, 'we'll insist they leave
tonight. I don't want them rattlesnakes
in town any longer.'

'They won't offer to leave,' Reece
said ruefully.

O'Brien nodded. 'I agree. So be
ready for anything.'

It was just five minutes later when
the three of them arrived outside the
saloon. They all stood there for a long
moment in silence, then climbed the

steps to the entrance and pushed through the slatted doors.

Provost and his top man Skinner were seated at a table in the center of the room, and were the only ones there. They hadn't opened the saloon for business. The two gunmen had been drinking, and there was a half-full bottle of Planters' Rye sitting on the table. Icepick was nowhere visible.

Provost and Skinner turned casually to the threesome at first, but then when they saw who they were, and that they were armed, both their faces went straight-lined.

'Look who's paying us a late visit,' Provost said carefully. 'What's going on, boys?'

'We come on over to hear your offer,' Smith spoke up for them.

'With those shotguns?' Provost said. 'Anyway, we was talking about tomorrow night. We're still trying to figure out a best deal.'

'There ain't no best deal,' O'Brien growled at him.

Provost gave him a steel-hard look. 'I knew you'd be trouble.'

Just at that moment, Icepick came in from a back room, carrying a case of ale. He stopped in his tracks, looked the situation over, and went over and deposited the case on the bar. He then moved up nearer to the others, staying close by the bar. 'What's going on here?'

Reece went over and leaned on the bar not far from Icepick, giving him a wary look.

'These boys say they want to talk tonight,' Provost said. 'They must be real eager to sell that Express company.' He managed a tight grin.

'You got it all wrong, Provost,' Smith said. 'But we wanted to give you the courtesy of hearing you out.'

'Well, then, put the shotguns down and set with us. This is a friendly palaver. Ain't it?'

'We'll keep the shotguns,' O'Brien told him. 'Just have your say and get on with it. We want to get some sleep tonight.'

'Maybe you'd like a long sleep,' Icepick grinned from the bar.

Skinner shot him a dark look.

'Don't pay him no mind,' Provost said. 'He takes to jumping ahead too far. If you take my meaning.'

'We understand you, you bastard!' Reece blurted out.

They all looked at him. Icepick chuckled in his throat.

'Is that all you got to say?' Smith asked angrily.

'No, it isn't. To avoid any more trouble between us, I'm willing to double our previous offer. One thousand dollars in hard cash. In gold if you want it. I can have it in forty-eight hours. And you'll never get a better offer.' He swigged down a half-glass of Planters'. 'I suggest you give it some very serious thought.'

Smith caught O'Brien's eye, then answered. 'I just did. We wouldn't sell the Express to you for twice what it's worth.'

'So,' O'Brien concluded for them, 'I

reckon that means you boys will be riding on out of here. Like you said you would. We'd appreciate it if you'd saddle up tonight.'

Provost rose from his chair, and stepped away from the table. Skinner stood up, too, moving his gunhand out, and Icepick turned toward the new action. Reece swallowed back his tension and pushed off the bar.

'You're getting right in my craw, hunter,' Provost spat out.

Reece recalled all he had heard about Provost, and tried to say something that would abort what was happening. 'I wouldn't get crossways of O'Brien, Provost.'

Nobody replied to that, but Skinner laughed out loud.

Provost looked over at Smith. 'I get the feeling that you'd've sold if this trail bum wasn't in this,' he said coolly. 'Why don't you and that moron at the bar just bow out and go off to bed? We'll talk to O'Brien separately.'

Smith shook his head. 'You are stupid,

210

Provost. O'Brien and me thought the same about this from the first. And nobody's leaving here but you.'

Provost made a face. 'Do you think you can stand up to us with those shotguns? You'll be sucking air through little round holes in you before you can pull triggers on those scatter-guns.'

O'Brien took a firm grip on the trigger assembly of his Remington. 'Then why don't you prove it?' he said in a half-whisper.

Tension filled the room up like a black thundercloud. Then, faster than the eye could follow, Provost made the first move.

The Colt Army .45 jumped out of its holster like it had been in his hand all the time, and the room resounded with its report. The gun was aimed at O'Brien's chest, because the gang had agreed that O'Brien had to be taken down first. But O'Brien had been watching Provost's eyes, as he had had to watch the eyes of animals on the hunt, to assess their next move. He had started a fall into a deep crouch as the shotgun muzzle came up to fire. Provost's shot tore at O'Brien's collar a half-inch from his jugular, creasing his neck there, as the Remington roared in the room, blasting Provost in the face and almost decapitating him. He was thrown violently off his feet, arms flung wide, slapping Skinner's shoulder as Skinner's Dardick barked out twice, missing Smith's head by inches and then striking him in the high chest with the second chunk of hot lead. Smith's shotgun exploded in an ear-ringing blast a half-second later, almost tearing Skinner in half at the waist. He took the table and a chair over with him as he thudded to the floor not far from Provost, whose body was still twitching there.

Icepick and Reece had drawn at the same time as Skinner, and both guns cracked out under the noise of the shotgun. Icepick's slug hit Reece just under the heart, but Reece still had the strength to return fire and blow a blue hole in Icepick's low chest. Icepick went down, and Reece fell against the bar and then slid slowly to the floor, eyes wide in the rictus of death.

O'Brien and Smith were still standing, but Smith had staggered back to lean against the bar not far from Reece.

The air was so thick with gunsmoke that it was hard to see through it for a couple moments, and it laid an iron taste on the tongue.

O'Brien looked over at Smith. 'You hit bad?'

Smith shook his head. 'I'll make it, partner. But Reece is gone.'

O'Brien walked over to Provost, who was a bloody mess. His head hung to one side, unrecognizable. O'Brien grated out a few words. 'No shooting awards this time, hotshot.'

Skinner's trousers were wet at the crotch, and he lay in a pool of crimson. He wasn't laughing any more. He was lifeless, mouth ajar in an expression of complete disbelief.

'That one is still alive,' Smith grunted

out, gesturing at Icepick.

A muffled sound came from Icepick as O'Brien walked over to him and stood over him, shotgun still in hand. Icepick glared up at O'Brien with hatred.

'That's right, you didn't kill me, you bastards. And you won't murder me in cold blood. It ain't in you. So get me a medic. Your partner over there will insist, hunter. But I don't forget. I'll be back some day when you don't expect me.' A tic marred his grin. 'You won't know when it happens. Then I'll find that little female you killed Latham over, and do things with her you ain't never heard of. After that I'll blow up that depot so there won't be no evidence you boys was ever here. What do you think of that?'

O'Brien casually aimed the shotgun at Icepick's chest and squeezed the second trigger of the big gun. There was a last deafening roar and flash, and Icepick jumped bodily, eyes wide, a melon-size hole in his chest from front to back. A rattling came from deep in his throat, and he quivered and died.

When O'Brien turned back to Smith, he was nodding his approval.

'I guess he shouldn't've mentioned Sarah,' he grinned, as O'Brien came to examine his wound.

O'Brien didn't respond. Smith had said it all.

9

It was early the next morning when Avery Spencer looked up from his desk and saw Sarah and Abigail arriving for their short work day. He had been tense about their coming ever since Old Scratch had woken him up at midnight to tell him what had happened at the Stage Trail Saloon.

'Morning, ladies,' he greeted them. 'You're in a little early today.'

'Abigail had some old tax records to look over, so I thought I might as well come in with her,' Sarah told him. She looked very pretty that morning. But she was more somber, since her last meeting with O'Brien.

'I've been trying to get at this for a week now,' Abigail said, removing her shawl and seating herself at a desk.

Spencer sneaked a look of assessment toward Sarah as she sat down too, at a third desk nearby.

'Did you ladies sleep well?' he started awkwardly.

Sarah gave him a quizzical look. 'Yes, thanks.'

'I always sleep well,' Abigail smiled. 'Ever since I was a youngster. My mother used to tell me — '

'Did you hear what happened last night?' he interrupted her in a rush.

Both women stared at him. Then Sarah got a little chill through her, thinking of O'Brien. She knew there was trouble with the Tulsa gunslingers. She found her breath coming short. 'What happened?' she said, dry-mouthed.

Spencer cleared his throat to continue. He knew women hated to hear about these things. It made them think less of their town. And their security.

'There was a big shoot-out. At the new saloon.'

Sarah's ears began ringing, and she thought for a moment she might fall off her chair.

'Who was involved?' Abigail asked casually.

'It was Smith and O'Brien,' Spencer continued. 'And one of the drivers. Reece, I think. They went up against those outlaws from Tulsa.

'One of our townsfolk was passing by. He said he never heard such a commotion in his life. Shotguns. Sidearms. You know of course that that Provost was an expert marksman.'

Sarah's cheeks were flushed, but she felt cold at the same time. She rose heatedly from her chair.

'Well, what happened, Mayor? Was anybody killed?'

He was surprised by her emotional outburst. 'Oh. Sorry. All the outlaws are dead. They're burying them in a common grave this morning.'

'What about our people?' Sarah fairly shouted at him.

He stared at her a brief moment. 'Right. Well, Reece was killed. Shot right through the heart, poor fellow.'

Now Abigail stepped in for her friend. 'O'Brien,' she said patiently. 'She wants to know about O'Brien, Mayor.'

Spencer's face changed. 'Oh, of course. He was shot, I hear.'

'Oh, God,' Sarah muttered, and put a hand to her hot cheek.

'It isn't a bad wound,' Spencer said quickly. 'Just a graze in his neck. But the vet says if he'd moved a half-inch, he'd be dead.'

Sarah began sobbing heavily, not able to control herself. Abigail got up and went over to her, and held her.

Spencer didn't know what to do or say. 'Smith was hit in the ribs, but he'll be OK,' he mumbled.

'Couldn't you have told it a little better than that?' Abigail scolded him, still comforting Sarah.

The sobs tapered off then, and Sarah took a handkerchief and dabbed at her pretty green eyes. 'I'm all right.'

'I . . . don't think I knew,' Spencer finally managed. 'I mean, about Sarah's feelings. For the hunter.'

'You must be the only one,' Abigail said sourly.

Spencer nodded thoughtfully. 'Does

O'Brien know about this?'

'That bear-man has no idea,' Abigail said angrily. 'She would have to hit him over the head with a club to get his attention. He doesn't have feelings, so he doesn't know the rest of us do.'

'Please, Abigail,' Sarah said, getting herself under control. 'I don't like it when you talk like that. Would he have brought me all the way from Kansas when he found me alone out there if he had no feelings? I owe him my life. Look what happened when that gunman attacked me.'

'Don't confuse gratitude with affection,' Spencer offered.

Sarah turned away 'I've never said I love him!' she said a bit too loudly. 'Isn't that right, Abigail?'

Abigail nodded. 'That's right, dear.'

'Where is Smitty?' Sarah asked him then. 'I want to see him. Maybe take him some soup or something.'

'Right. Smitty,' Spencer said. 'I think he's back at the depot. Got a big bandage on his side, but feeling good.'

'I'll get my work done later today,' Sarah said. 'I'll just walk over there.'

'Of course, Sarah. We'll see you when you get back.'

Sarah left then, and arrived at the depot a few minutes later. There were a couple of drivers out back, but Smith was alone in his office.

'Oh, God. There you are,' she said, her eyes watering up. She went over and hugged him and put a big smile on his face.

'What did I do to deserve that?' In his booming voice.

'Are you hurt badly?'

'No, no. It was a through and through. I'm just a little stiff in the side.' He moved his arm and grimaced in pain. 'Of course, O'Brien is treating me like a damn patient.'

She looked around. 'Where is he?'

'Oh, he took that Appaloosa of his out for some exercise. Acts like nothing happened last night. He's got a bandage on his neck, but he's fine. Fought the vet about that bandage. I thought it would be a wrestling match for a minute there.' A soft laugh.

Sarah sat down on a chair near him. 'You like him, don't you?'

He blew his fat cheeks out. 'O'Brien and me go back a long way, Sarah. Had us many a hunt together. He saved my life at least once, maybe more. That puts something between you that can't wear out. I'd trust that man with my life or my life savings. You can count on him. Yes, I like him. He's probably the best friend I ever made.'

Sarah sat there thinking about that. 'That's the way I feel.'

'You feel more than that, darling,' he said quietly.

She looked over at him, and sighed. 'He's lived alone too long,' she said. 'He'll never take on a woman, Smitty. The idea is entirely alien to him. And that's not his fault. It's part of who he is, and I wouldn't want to change him at all. He's a kind of marvelous human being.'

Smith shook his head. 'You got it

bad. I'm real sorry for you, Sarah. I mean it.' He paused. 'I told you before, I'm going to lose him, too.'

She looked forlorn. 'Are you sure?'

'There are signs. He don't like this life, Sarah. Fort Revenge is like a kind of prison to a man like him. We just have to let the wild thing in him have its way. That's the way things are.'

'If he leaves, I will, too,' she said.

Smith sat there. 'That would be a big loss for this town. And for me.'

She smiled at him. 'It was O'Brien who made me think this was a nice place to settle in. With him gone, this would just be a backwoods town a long way from home.'

'Well. I hear you. What I won't never understand is that boy's blindness to what's right in front of him. You'd be the best thing that happened to him since he left the mountains back east as a kid.'

'That's kind, Smitty,' she said, her eyes moist.

'And that's another thing. Who's

going to call me Smitty when you're both gone?'

She gave him a lovely smile. 'I'll miss you. A lot.'

★ ★ ★

Later that day, with Smith feeling better, O'Brien decided to go out small-game hunting, and Smith insisted on going with him, over O'Brien's protests.

Through that warm afternoon they shot three rabbits, a fox, and a couple of game birds. Then they pitched hardship camp at the same place they had previously when they went trapping together, alongside a small river. The stream was a rushing torrent now because of rain up farther, and it made a dull roaring sound near them. Smith was feeling the wound, but kept it to himself.

The rabbits were skinned and gutted and hung out to dry in the late sun. It was too early to eat, but they shared a pot of coffee boiled over their open fire.

'Say, you know something? I remembered this back in town. I forgot to check one of them beaver traps last time we was out here. There could be something in there.'

'Forget it,' O'Brien said. 'That river could've washed the whole thing downstream by now.'

'No, by Jesus!' Smith bellowed. 'I might have me a real nice catch there. I'm going to check it. Come on, partner. You can help.'

He got up from a stump, and made a face. He still had a thick bandage on his chest and side, and was loaded up with laudanum to keep the pain clown.

O'Brien stood, too. 'I wouldn't't've let you come out here if I'd known you'd be trapping,' O'Brien told him. 'You ain't in no shape for that.'

'Oh, I'm fine,' Smith argued, his eyes still showing hurt from standing. 'The wound ain't hardly weeping now. Come on, this will take two minutes.'

O'Brien reluctantly followed him

along the river's edge where the water was roaring past loudly. Finally Smith stopped. 'Here. This is it. I can see it in there.'

'You'd have to go in the water,' O'Brien said. 'Let it go.'

But Smith had to prove he was all right. Before O'Brien could protest further, he had stepped into the wild current, reaching for the trap that showed from under the surface. And a moment after that, his feet were swept out from under him and he was being carried downstream. 'Hey!' he yelled out.

O'Brien knew Smith couldn't swim, and would drown in this violent current. In the next second he had dived into the water, caught up to Smith, and grabbed him by his shirt. Smith was flailing wildly, grabbing at O'Brien. But O'Brien fought the current and his friend and dragged him to shore downstream fifty yards.

They lay on the mud together, trying to breathe. They had both lost their hats, and were dripping wet. O'Brien looked over at him. 'You goddamn old jackass.'

Smith was gasping for air. 'Well, you ... done it again. Saved me from them ... Pearly Gates. With you around I might just live forever.'

'What the hell are you trying to prove?' he bit out angrily.

Smith shrugged. 'I guess I don't want to admit that Provost could put a crimp in my routine. I was wrong.'

'You got it bleeding again,' O'Brien said heavily. 'Come on, let's get back to camp.'

They were back in camp in ten minutes. O'Brien got some gauze and tape out from his saddle-bag and re-bandaged Smith's side. The wound had survived the strenuous dunking rather well, and O'Brien was relieved.

'It's funny. I was just telling Sarah how you saved my life out hunting.'

'I didn't save your life,' O'Brien said curtly. 'That fat on you would've let you float clear to the Gulf of Mexico.'

Smith looked over at him. 'Sorry,

partner. And thanks.'

'For God's sake,' O'Brien spat out.

They sat by the crackling fire in their long underwear. O'Brien threw another chunk of wood on it. The sky was getting dark overhead.

'Just like old times, ain't it?' Smith finally ventured.

'Nothing is like old times,' O'Brien said. 'So you and Sarah was talking.'

Smith looked over at him. 'Yes. She was worried over you.' He watched O'Brien's face.

'Do you think she'll be OK? I mean, in Fort Revenge. The Territory.'

That was the first concern Smith had ever heard O'Brien utter about Sarah.

'I reckon that depends on circumstances.'

O'Brien turned to him. 'What circumstances?'

'Oh, I guess who's around her, and who ain't.' Another look.

O'Brien sat there on his saddle for a long while as dark settled in. 'Smitty. This might be a bad time to bring this up, but I don't think I can do this.'

Smith sighed a heavy sigh. 'It ain't like I didn't know. But now I wish you'd never come down here. It will be too hard when you're gone.'

O'Brien regarded him soberly. The fact was, he would miss Smith's company, too. It had been good, riding the trail with him. Sitting at a camp-fire together. Enjoying their luck with the traps.

'I know,' he finally said.

'Are you sure you've give the company a fair chance?' Smith suggested. 'There's a lot of people that like you here.' Hoping he thought of Sarah.

'You know I ain't no bookkeeper,' O'Brien said. 'I can't hardly read the bills of lading. Or the schedules.'

'Sarah was going to teach you about reading,' Smith said.

'That might be a little like teaching a bear to eat with a fork and knife,' O'Brien responded.

Smith looked over at him, and he was grinning slightly.

'You made any going-away plans?' Smith wondered.

'Not yet. I want to watch that side of yours a while. Get it straight in my head what I want to do, and where I want to do it.'

'You only know two things,' Smith said. 'Hunting and trapping.'

O'Brien nodded. 'I doubt I'd take up bank clerking.'

Smith grinned. After a long moment, he decided to take a risk.

'I know you warned me about this, but I got to have my say, if you're leaving us. What about Sarah?'

O'Brien turned to him with a heavy frown. 'Do you want me to shoot you in that other side?'

Smith looked at the ground. 'I can't help it. That girl's whole future depends on what you do next. She's attached to you, O'Brien.'

O'Brien tried to relax about it. 'All right. Let's have it out. I brought her here from Kansas, and that put something between us. Like a doctor who saves a patient. There's a feeling that develops because of what the doctor did for him. That's all it is, Smitty. Even though she might think different for a while now. Can you imagine any woman feeling anything much for me? I ain't woman material, partner. Never will be. No woman would want to follow me around. It ain't a woman's life. I don't have to tell you that.'

'I think Sarah might have different ideas about all that,' Smith pursued. 'You said she handled that trip south like a trooper. You told me she had grit. You don't know what she'd do till you ask her.'

O'Brien shook his head. 'I don't know what you're thinking, old friend. That laudanum must've frazzled what brain you got left. Jumping in that river like that. No, don't start imagining things that could never happen. And don't bring it up again. I think we've said everything that had to be said.'

Smith was unhappy and tired. 'Right. Whatever you say, buffalo man.'

* ★ ★ ★

The sun had spilled a lavish array of
pastel hues on to the eastern horizon
that next morning. In Fort Revenge,
citizens were just waking up to the
perfect summer day with the expecta-
tion of tranquility, now that the town
had been rid of Frank Provost and his
men. But at mid-morning, two men
rode into town who had no interest in
preserving the peace and quiet. Ezra
and Matt Logan walked their mounts
slowly into town, dark-visaged and
ominous-looking.

They saw the Stage Trail Saloon, and
reined up in front of it.

'Well,' Ezra said tiredly. 'This is it.
This is where he's supposed to be. I see
a boarding-house down the street.
That's good for us.'

'I ain't had a decent drink in days,'
young Matt complained. 'Let's wet our
whistles in this excuse for a saloon.'

'Every once in a while you get a good
idea, son,' Ezra grinned.

They tied their mounts to the hitching post outside, and went in.

There was nobody there. They went up to the bar and Ezra pounded on it. 'Hey! Anybody there? You got customers out here!'

In a moment Thatcher came in from the back room with a broom. 'Oh. Good morning, boys. Sorry, but the saloon hasn't reopened yet.'

'Reopened?' Matt said sourly.

'Oh, we had us a big gunfight in here a coupla nights ago. Four men buried at Boot Hill yesterday. We never seen nothing like it.'

Ezra and Matt looked casually at each other.

'The law caught up with some bandits?' Ezra conjectured.

'No, we don't have any law. It was outsiders against locals. See them stains on the floor over there? That's the blood of outlaws.' Thatcher had taken over the saloon again now that Provost was gone. He had torn up the sale agreement.

Matt looked around to see the stains, but Ezra kept his gaze fixed on Thatcher. 'Did you lose any of your boys?'

'A stage driver, yes. But Smith and O'Brien come through it OK.'

Matt turned back quickly to the bar. 'O'Brien?' he said.

Ezra gave him a slow look. Thatcher nodded.

'He's new here. But a tougher boy you'll never meet. Him and Smith cleaned this town up for us.'

They had heard something like that in Sulphur Creek. 'Sounds like this O'Brien is a man that looks for trouble,' Ezra commented.

'Why, I don't think so. But he don't shy away from it neither.'

Ezra grunted out his disdain. 'We'll take two Cuban rums, barkeep.'

'I told you: we're closed. I got a lot of clean-up to do in here.'

'And I told you,' Ezra said in a quiet voice that made a little chill ripple through Thatcher. 'We want two rums.

If you ain't got it, make it whiskey.'

Thatcher swallowed hard. 'Are you boys from Tulsa?'

Ezra gave him a burning look. 'Bring the drinks.'

Thatcher nodded. 'OK. I think I got a bottle of rum on the shelves somewhere.'

Thatcher brought the bottle, poured out two glasses of it, and left the bottle. 'If you boys are with Frank Provost I didn't have nothing to do with that shoot-out. I was over at my café across the street.'

'We'll be stopping over there later. You got ham and eggs there?'

'Sure,' Thatcher said.

Ezra swigged his drink and poured himself another one. 'Just as a matter of curiosity, where would I find this O'Brien? To give him a pat on the back for, you know, a good job.'

'Oh, he's out of town,' Thatcher said. 'Him and Smith went out hunting yesterday. Might be back later today.'

'Does he have a place here?' Matt

pursued it too quickly.

Thatcher didn't notice Ezra's sigh. 'He's got a cabin out on the north road. But he sleeps at the depot sometimes.'

Ezra nodded. 'Well, I hope we run into him while we're here.'

Thatcher's face belied his curiosity. 'I guess you boys got business here, then?'

'Oh, no,' Ezra said casually. 'We're on our way to Tulsa. We just need a little rest for a coupla days. Does that rooming-house have any space available?'

'You'll have to ask Mrs Barstow. But she usually does.'

Ezra tossed some coins on to the bar. 'Thanks for opening up,' he said with acidity. 'You'll see us at your diner.'

Thatcher grinned a relaxed grin. 'I hope so, gentlemen.'

A few minutes later they had walked their horses down to Mrs Barstow's. They found her in the large parlor as they walked in, and made arrangements for a room for two nights.

'We'll be glad to have you,' Mrs Barstow told them.

Over on a wall beside a bay window, Sarah was sitting in a soft chair while she read an item from the Tulsa newspaper that reported an American named Henry Stanley was setting up Belgian trading posts in the Congo, and that a rapid-firing 'machine-gun' had been invented by a Londoner named Maxim. She looked up for a moment and Matt was staring at her. She looked back down, embarrassed.

She had been seriously thinking of packing up her things in preparation for leaving town, regardless of what O'Brien did.

'I'll just get you a receipt,' Mrs Barstow was saying to Ezra. 'Would you step into this ante-room for a moment?'

Ezra went with her and Matt sidled over to Sarah.

'Morning, sweetheart. What's a looker like you doing in a back-country territory like this?'

Sarah glanced up at him, still distracted by thoughts of her immediate future. 'Good morning,' she replied coolly. 'Right now I'm trying to read this article in the paper. If you'll excuse me.' She went back to the paper.

He was not dissuaded. 'Do you live here?'

She looked up again, in irritation. And the thought came to her in a flashing moment that when she left this place, there would never again be an O'Brien to step in and protect her from unpleasant men.

'I believe that would be none of your business,' she said bluntly.

He grinned at her. 'Woo-ee! Did I get my ears pinned back!'

Sarah rose from her chair. 'I have work waiting for me down the street. I hope you have a pleasant stay here.'

He doffed his hat as she moved around him and out the front door. Ezra arrived back at that same moment. 'I got the room,' he said. 'Say, what was you doing there?'

'Just admiring the local scenery. Did you see that delicious little morsel that just walked out?'

Ezra gave him a scathing look.

'I was only looking, Ezra.'

'Go get that stuff from our saddle-bags. We'll bed the horses down later. Meet me in room 23.'

Five minutes later they were settled into their room, with Ezra flopped on to the iron bed, propped up on a pillow.

'I could sleep for a week,' he admitted. 'I might not make the noon meal. The riding kinks got my legs all knotted up.'

'Then I'll go alone,' Matt said, looking out a window on to the street, hoping to see Sarah out there. 'I could eat a bull moose.'

Ezra saw what he was doing. 'Do you even remember why we rode all the way down here, boy?'

Matt came from the window and seated himself on an overstuffed chair across the room. 'Don't insult me, Gramps. I want that sonofabitch every bit as much as you.'

'Then act like it. Leave the damn women alone while this is going on.'

'Sorry, Ezra.'

'You look at another one, I'll use my goddamn gunbelt on you.'

Matt decided it was best not to respond.

'Now. What's coming up here ain't no bank robbery. There's no room for failure. It's the family name, you understand?'

'Of course. I expect to fill that hunter up with so much lead they won't be able to lift him into a casket.'

Ezra swung his legs off the bed. 'Listen to me, and listen good. We'll probably only get one shot at this. It has to work the first time. Get that in your head.'

'I'm no dummy, Ezra'

'Then prove it, by Jesus. Follow my lead. If it's possible, I want him to go slow. Real slow. Look at this like it's a military operation and I'm the goddamn general.'

'You're the general.'

'When we leave this stinkhole of a town, I want that hunter so shot up his own mother wouldn't recognize him.'

'It's as good as done.' Across the room, Matt grinned, staring into that future.

10

O'Brien and Shanghai Smith arrived back in town late afternoon, with Smith bleeding through his new bandage. O'Brien was angry with him.

'You never did know how to take care of yourself, damn you,' he told Smith, when they arrived at the local veterinarian's office. There was no doctor yet in town, although one rode through occasionally, so sickness and injury had to be attended to by the animal doctor. He was the one who had given Smith laudanum, which made Smith feel better than he actually was. Now the drug was out of his system and he was feeling plenty of pain from the incident on the river.

O'Brien wouldn't help him off his mount, or walk him into the building. He figured Smith didn't deserve any special attention.

The vet had just finished delivering a

calf at the back of the house, and had to wash up before he could look at Smith's wound. O'Brien went into the exam room with them, and stood in a corner.

'Yeah, you got it opened up, all right,' the vet told Smith, as he unwrapped the bandage O'Brien had put on at their camp. 'Let's see what it looks like.' He was a slim, wiry fellow with wire-rim spectacles and a toupee that kept sliding forward toward his forehead.

'Just slap another bandage on it, Doc, and I'll get out of your way.'

'Jesus,' O'Brien muttered. 'Don't pay no attention to him. He ain't been in his right mind for some time.' He had recovered his Stetson downstream from where he dragged Smith ashore, and it sat on his head, crumpled and weathered-looking. Smith hadn't been as lucky and was bare-headed, showing a balding head of graying hair.

'This isn't bad,' the vet finally commented. 'You start treating it right, it'll heal up in a few days.'

'See? What did I tell you, partner? I

been stung by bees worse than this!'

O'Brien shook his head. 'See what I mean?'

'You have to take care of this now, Mr Smith. A coupla days of rest will help a lot. Nothing physical,' he said, as he re-wrapped the wound. 'I'll give you another swig of laudanum before you leave. That should last till it feels better. Come back and see me day after tomorrow.'

Smith got off the examination table and pulled on a shirt. 'In two days I'll be ready to tame mustangs!' he grinned.

'Maybe you could put him to sleep for a week,' O'Brien suggested sourly.

Smith belted out a laugh. 'Say, take a look at O'Brien's neck there, Doc.'

'You touch that scab on my neck and I'll shoot you,' O'Brien growled.

The vet shook his head, and the toupee came forward, requiring an adjustment. 'You two are a pair, all right. Are all buffalo hunters like this?'

'Well,' Smith said more seriously, 'this here boy is the worst of them. Got his leg busted once in a stampede. Set and splinted it hisself and never saw a doctor. Limped on it for three months. But he never quit hunting all that time.'

'Goddamn it, Smitty. Get your laudanum and let's get to hell out of here.'

Smith grinned as he rose. 'He's such a sweetheart.'

They walked their mounts down to the depot then, and R.C. Funk greeted them at the office. There were a couple moments of banter, then O'Brien and Smith went back to the bunk room and sat down facing each other.

'I'm going to ride out to the cabin,' O'Brien said quietly. 'I'll be sleeping out there tonight. I got some things to do.'

Smith furrowed his brow, regarding O'Brien seriously. 'You're getting ready to leave, ain't you.'

O'Brien nodded. 'Now that I know you'll be OK, there ain't much reason for me to delay my plans. Tomorrow I'll take the day clueing you in on what I've done to clutter up your books. The following day I'll be riding out.'

'North?'

O'Brien nodded. 'Probably where I come from when I rode down here.'

'I thought it was all over-worked up there.'

'A trapper come through here a few days ago, before our show-down with Provost. Just come from Colorado, and said the beaver have made a come-back in that area. Ermine, too. Hell, it can't be much worse than it is hereabouts.'

'Sorry I steered you wrong on that,' Smith said soberly. 'If it had been good here, you might have stayed.'

'I want you to keep my cash input,' O'Brien told him. 'I don't need it. I got a little sum in a Denver bank. And I want the Express to make good.'

Hard-as-nails Smith felt a small lump in his throat, and had to pause a moment before speaking. 'Much obliged, partner. I'll find a way to send you a share of any profits.'

'The hell you will,' O'Brien said. 'And I don't want no argument about this.'

Smith sighed, and nodded. He knew it was pointless to argue with O'Brien once he had made his mind up on something. 'I wish I could tell you I'm happy about this. I saw us having a great new life down here together. But I guess some things just ain't meant to be.'

'We always rode a good trail together,' O'Brien said softly. 'Frying salt pork on a green stick and happy to have it. Galloping through thick herds of prime buff. But them days is deader than thunder now.'

'When are you going to tell Sarah?'

O'Brien gave him a look, and sighed. 'Some time before I leave, Smitty.'

'You know she'll be gone soon after you.'

Smith had mentioned that possibility before. 'I hope that don't happen. She likes it here.'

'She likes it here with you,' Smith corrected him.

O'Brien rose, shaking his head. 'Let's not get into that again. I'll see you early tomorrow. I want to leave you in good

247

shape. Take care of that side.'

He left Smith sitting there, looking sober. When he got outside and mounted the Appaloosa, there were two men standing in the street down by the saloon, watching with interest. It was Ezra and Matt Logan.

Ezra nudged Matt in the side. 'There. That's him.'

Matt swallowed hard. It was getting close. 'That's the assassin of my daddy, by God.'

O'Brien was riding past now. He took no notice of the two men. They acted like they were in conversation until he was gone.

'He don't look like much,' Matt said confidently. 'This might be easy, Ezra.'

'He's heading out to that cabin of his,' Ezra said, still looking after O'Brien. 'I doubt he'll be coming back in town tonight. When it gets dark, we're going out there.'

Matt looked over at him quickly. 'Tonight?'

'What's the matter, boy? Getting cold

feet?' He gave a hard grin.

Matt's face colored slightly. 'I told you. I'm ready.'

'Good. Then he won't live to see another sunrise.'

★   ★   ★

There was no moon that night. Crickets and cicadas rasped their songs out under a black-as-pitch sky when the Logans rode out to O'Brien's cabin.

They reined in a hundred yards away, so he wouldn't hear their horses, picketing the mounts under a cottonwood tree. O'Brien had corraled the Appaloosa out back, and there was kerosene lantern light coming from inside.

'This is good,' Ezra said quietly. 'That door probably ain't locked. We can surprise him real good if we do it right.'

Matt found himself quivering slightly inside. He was fast with his gun, but he had never actually killed a man yet. He had wounded a bank teller a year ago, but that fellow hadn't even been armed.

The stories he had heard about O'Brien began spinning through his head, and the cockiness was gone.

'Can I take him down, Ezra?' he said tensely. 'So I can say I killed O'Brien? It's something I could brag about my whole life. You're an old man.'

Ezra grabbed him by his shirt front. 'This ain't some goddamn bragging game we're playing here, boy! This is life-or-death stuff! It has to go off without a hitch. We have to get our shots in before he even knows we're there.'

'I can do that.'

Ezra ignored him. 'I'm going through that door first. I don't trust you to do it right; you're too green. That means I'll have the first shots. Then you can step in and pump him full of lead, if he ain't already down. If he is, wait till I tell you what to do. I'd prefer he go real slow. Kneecaps. Groin. I want to hear him yell in miserable pain.'

'Just so I get my chance at him,' Matt said, licking dry lips.

They moved slowly up to the cabin

until they were standing just outside its door. They had taken off their riding spurs where they picketed the horses so made no sound. They couldn't see what was going on inside because the window on the side of the cabin was translucent skin and Sarah had put up curtains over it.

Ezra put his finger to his lips, and they moved up right against the heavy wooden door. Ezra motioned and they both drew their guns. He reached forward and moved a door handle and the door unlatched silently.

Ezra glanced at Matt once more, took in a deep breath and eased the big door open. It swung silently on leather hinges.

O'Brien was across the room, his back to them, making up a bedroll for the Appaloosa's irons, preoccupied, thinking about Smith, and Sarah, mulling over what Smith had confided to him about Sarah. His Winchester was ten feet away.

Ezra stepped on to the floor of the cabin, and fired his Tranter .38 twice at O'Brien's back.

When Ezra had stepped on to the cabin floor, though, a very slight squeak had occurred, and O'Brien's keen sense of hearing had caught it. As Ezra fired, O'Brien was turning and bending, his right hand going for the skinning knife in his stovepipe boot.

Ezra's first shot, instead of hitting O'Brien in mid-back, struck him high on his left chest like a club, slamming him against the nearby wall. The second shot went wild, tearing at his right sleeve as O'Brien unsheathed the knife and hurled it at Ezra in one smooth motion.

The knife turned over twice in mid-air, and thudded into Ezra's chest just under his heart.

Both Ezra and Matt stared at the knife as if it had appeared magically in Ezra's chest. Matt froze with shock for a moment. Ezra tried unsuccessfully to pull the offending blade from its fatal resting place, then began toppling to the floor.

While he was falling, O'Brien was diving for the Winchester on the wall near him, as Matt began firing at him furiously, shooting fast but not accurately. The first two slugs smacked into the wall and floor beside O'Brien's chest and legs, and a third struck him in the right thigh as he grabbed the rifle in a swift motion and turned it on Matt. The gun roared in the room and hurled Matt against the open door, hit in the low ribs. O'Brien cocked and re-aimed, and Matt threw his Iver-Johnson to the floor as if it were a snake that had bitten him.

'Don't kill me!' Matt cried out in new terror.

'Why the hell not?' O'Brien grated out. His finger tightened on the trigger.

'No, please! I ain't no good at this! I wish I'd never come.'

O'Brien stood up, the rifle still aimed at Matt's heart. He was bleeding through his rawhide tunic over his left chest, and there was a hot burning on his right thigh.

'Who the hell are you?' O'Brien demanded.

'We're the Logans. That's my grand-daddy you just killed.' He looked down fearfully at Ezra, who had died on the floor, O'Brien's skinning knife still sticking out of his chest.

'For God's sake, you people.' He walked over to Matt, feeling the pain now in his chest. 'How many of you are there, damn it?'

Matt licked dry lips. 'We're the last. Really. And I promise you, this is over now. I'd never try anything like this again. Just let me live. I'm young. I want to see thirty.' His side was bleeding through his shirt.

O'Brien leaned the rifle on the wall near them, then came back over and back-handed Matt across the face, knocking two teeth out of his jaw. Matt spat out teeth and blood, and started to slip to the floor. O'Brien grabbed him and held him very close.

'I want you to get your mounts, put him on his, and ride out of here. Tonight.'

'I need medical help.'

'Do you want to live?'

Matt nodded groggily.

'Then you do what I tell you. I'll help you get him loaded. Get your ribs looked at somewhere else. It ain't a bad wound.'

Matt spat some more blood out.

'Now, listen carefully: if I ever see your mangey hide again, you're a dead man.'

Matt coughed weakly. 'I understand.'

O'Brien's wound was high, just under his shoulder, but the lead had not struck bone. With his good right arm he dragged Ezra out to the horses and helped get him aboard his mount. Then Matt was on his way, riding glumly off into the night.

* * *

It was hard saddling the Appaloosa with one good arm. But a half-hour after Matt Logan's humble departure with his grandfather's corpse, O'Brien was knocking on the vet's door.

'Oh, my God! You again? What is it with you people?'

255

'Never mind,' O'Brien said acidly. 'Just fix this shoulder up. I'm going to be needing it soon.'

He was still on the exam table when Smith came busting in, face flushed. 'They told me you was here! What the hell happened?'

'Oh, a couple more Logans found me. It's all over, Smitty. One dead, the other gone with his tail between his legs. I'm all right.'

'Like hell you are!' the vet said. 'I'll make you a sling for that shoulder after I get it plugged up. The bullet went through.'

'What about his leg?' Smith said.

'That's just a flesh wound,' the vet replied. 'But he won't use that left arm for quite a spell.'

'I wish we could count on that,' Smith said sourly.

'You're one to talk,' O'Brien muttered. 'Come on, Doc, hurry this up. I got better things to do.'

Smith and the vet exchanged a look just as Sarah rushed into the room, out

256

of breath. Eyes full of fear. 'Oh, God! You're alive! I thought — '

She began sobbing.

Smith went to her and touched her shoulder. 'Hey. It's OK. He'll be all right.'

'He'll heal up in a few weeks,' the vet assured her, showing surprise at her reaction. He stepped away from O'Brien, and then Sarah caused more surprise. She strode over to O'Brien and hit him twice on the chest. Fiercely.

'Damn you! You can't keep doing this to me! I'm glad you're going! I'm really glad!'

O'Brien was just sitting there stunned. Sarah turned, still sobbing, and hurried from the house.

The room fell silent. O'Brien grew a mild frown on his square face as Smith went over to him. 'See what I mean?' he smiled.

The vet was shaking his head. He examined the new bandage he had just applied. 'No, she didn't hurt the wound. She's a real hell cat, isn't she? Is that your woman?'

O'Brien didn't even hear him. He was still staring, bewildered, after Sarah.

'No, she ain't,' Smith said soberly, giving O'Brien a dark look.

'Well, what the hell,' O'Brien finally murmured to himself.

In the next few moments the vet had applied a sling to O'Brien's shoulder and arm. 'Now you keep that on there for a couple of weeks. You can even sleep with it on. It will help you heal.'

O'Brien muttered an acknowledgment, still trying to understand what had happened.

'How is that side of yours, Mr Smith? Much bleeding or weeping through that last bandage?'

'No, I'm just fine,' Smith told him. But he grimaced when he moved. 'Well, why don't we walk on down to the depot, partner? I'd like to hear more about them Logans.'

O'Brien looked up at him distractedly. 'Tell you what, I'll meet you down there a little later, Smitty. I want a minute alone here.'

Smith furrowed his brow. 'Sure. I'll see you down there.'

'You can sit there as long as you like,' the vet told O'Brien. 'I'll go make some notes on your wound. Would you like a swig of laudanum before you go?'

'Hell, no,' O'Brien said testily.

O'Brien sat there for almost ten minutes, staring at the opposite wall, before he finally got up and left. His shoulder hurt a lot now, and he had to limp slightly on his right leg. Outside, he walked his horse on down the street toward the depot. But at Mrs Barstow's house he stopped short, and stared at a lighted window he knew to be Sarah's.

Then he tethered the Appaloosa to a hitching rail and went in.

When he painfully climbed the stairs and knocked on Sarah's door, there was no response for a couple of moments, then the door swung open and she stood inside, looking a bit disheveled, her dark hair hanging in wisps alongside her face.

'Oh. It's you. I know I owe you an

apology. I don't know what's the matter with me.'

'I think maybe I do,' he said quietly. 'Mind if I come in a few minutes?'

'Well, I was actually starting to prepare for bed,' she said awkwardly. 'I'm sure we'll see each other before you leave.' She averted her pretty eyes.

O'Brien sighed. 'I kind of wanted to talk now, Sarah. I'm not sure I can say what I want to, later.'

She shrugged. 'All right, Just for a few minutes.'

He stepped past her and could smell a fragrance that was very pleasant. Like desert blossoms. She went over and stood beside her bed, away from him; he leaned on the wall near the door.

'Mrs Barstow probably wouldn't approve,' she said with a forced smile.

O'Brien nodded and grinned. He removed his Stetson and ran a hand through thick, slightly graying hair. 'Sarah, I think you know I plan to leave Fort Revenge day after tomorrow.'

She felt a heaviness inside her. She

felt like crying again, but pushed it back. 'Yes. I know. And I wish you well. I hope you make a life again that you've been yearning for. You deserve it.'

He pushed off the wall, and grimaced.

'You're hurting.' She wanted to rush over and examine the bandage under the sling, but restrained herself.

'I'll feel better after a good night's sleep.'

'Who shot you? More of Provost's men?'

'It was a revenge shooting. Couple of crazies from up north. But it's all over now.' He fixed his gaze on hers. 'You don't have to worry your head no more about it.'

She turned quickly away. 'What makes you think I'd worry?'

He grinned slightly. 'Anyway, I'm not leaving in two days.'

She turned back to him.

'I'm leaving tomorrow.'

A renewed anger showed itself in her green eyes and she turned away again. 'Fine! Maybe you'd like to say goodbye now. It will be less trouble for you.'

O'Brien sighed again. He had trouble putting things well when he spoke to women. 'What I'm saying is, I liked what you done in there. At the vet.'

She turned back, still somber.

'I don't think I knew your mind till that moment,' he admitted. 'I think you got a soft spot for me, Sarah Carter.'

Her face changed. Several emotions flooded through her. 'Well! So that's the way you see it?'

He nodded. 'And now it seems I got one for you. What I come here to say is, when I ride out of here tomorrow, I want you with me.'

Sarah stood transfixed in shock. 'What?'

'That's right. I been thinking. There'd be a big hole in my world now if you wasn't in it. It took a long time for me to realize that. Sorry.'

'You want me to ride north with you?' The unbelievable reality was just sinking in.

'I know it's a lot to ask, trying to make a home out in the mountains of

Colorado with a trail bum like me. But there's a trapper's cabin up there I could make into a real house. And a minister close by to make you respectable.'

Sarah's ears were ringing, and tears came without her knowing it. Suddenly she was running over to him and flinging her arms around his broad shoulders, and smothering him with kisses.

O'Brien was surprised and pleased. He held her warm, soft body close with his good arm, and liked it, his breath coming shallowly.

'I guess that means you'll go,' he managed.

She looked into his masculine, bearded face, the face that had come to symbolize safety for her ever since Kansas, and knew now that it would always be there for her. 'I wouldn't miss it for all the tea in Boston Harbor,' she told him, flashing a beautiful smile that warmed his insides.

★ ★ ★

The next morning, after a quick breakfast at the Prairie Café, O'Brien and Sarah stopped at the depot on their way out of town. A widely grinning Shanghai Smith hugged them both on his porch. He had been told the night before, and passed the whole night without sleep. But it was worth losing O'Brien to see this small miracle happen.

'You take care of this bull buffalo now, Sarah!' Smith boomed out jovially. 'He gets a little out of control sometimes.'

'I'll give it my best effort,' she smiled at him.

They were on their mounts a moment later, with O'Brien awkward because of the sling over his rawhides, Sarah on a chestnut gelding purchased last night from Thatcher.

'Make this the best damn stage line in the Territory,' O'Brien said quietly to his old friend.

'And you make that mountain country yours,' Smith answered.

O'Brien gave him a last, long look

and then he and Sarah rode off into their uncertain future.

But, from this moment forward, it would be together.

We do hope that you have enjoyed reading this large print book.

Did you know that all of our titles are available for purchase?

We publish a wide range of high quality large print books including:
Romances, Mysteries, Classics
General Fiction
Non Fiction and Westerns

Special interest titles available in large print are:
The Little Oxford Dictionary
Music Book, Song Book
Hymn Book, Service Book

Also available from us courtesy of Oxford University Press:
Young Readers' Dictionary
(large print edition)
Young Readers' Thesaurus
(large print edition)

For further information or a free brochure, please contact us at:
Ulverscroft Large Print Books Ltd.,
The Green, Bradgate Road, Anstey,
Leicester, LE7 7FU, England.
Tel: (00 44) **0116 236 4325**
Fax: (00 44) **0116 234 0205**

Other titles in the
Linford Western Library:

THE GAMBLERS OF WASTELAND

Jim Lawless

Convinced that Blackjack Chancer is behind the death of their youngest brother, Lukus and Kris Rheingold devise a plan. Lukus steals the Saturday-night takings from Chancer's casino, Wasteland Eldorado, and Kris outwits the Marshal and the Wasteland posse as they track him. The Rheingold brothers head for home, followed by the mysterious Lil Lavender, and later by Chancer and his hired gun, Fallon. All three have their reasons for hunting Lukus — and the hunt leads to a final bloody climax in the Rheingold family cemetery.

MACAHAN'S LAW

Steve Hayes

When a lonely way station is attacked by the notorious Colbert gang, the marshal stops a bullet in the fight. Young Ezra Macahan finds himself with a heavy responsibility. The marshal's dying words: 'Take the Colbert brothers into Santa Rosa and turn 'em over to the sheriff.' It's a tall order, and Ezra will have to fight every step of the way to get it done. The final showdown sees Macahan go from boy to man . . . and from man to lawman.

THE TRAIL TO TRINITY

Owen G. Irons

The Trail to Trinity is rugged, and dangerous as hell. Sage Paxton rides it only out of the direst of necessities — to avenge his murdered parents. Sage has decided that their killer will not see another day. Bad weather, a lame horse, a crooked army officer, and outlaws will not keep him from his prize. Nothing else matters now, not even his own life. Before the end of the day, he will have vengeance against his parents' killer — and his own brother . . .

RIDE A SAVAGE LAND

Ian McDougall

Returning from the carnage of war, Will Raith struggles to settle back into ranch life. When a summons to ride to Laramie arises, Raith needs little persuasion to accept the mission, helping free the lands opening up in the West from greedy land-grabbers like the ruthless Jacob Rendell. But this is not a mission for a man alone. Before Raith faces Rendell and his hired guns, he will need help. And to get that help, he must first get himself imprisoned . . .

BAD BLOOD

Corba Sunman

Deputy US Marshal Cal Burnett rides into Pike's Peak, Kansas, after an absence of ten years, expecting to find the town as he had left it. Any hopes of this are quickly destroyed, though. Strange and disturbing rumours reach him: his brother, Lance, has disappeared, and people say he robbed the local bank before skipping town. Cal begins to investigate, but it's when he meets the local law — Sheriff Snark and his deputy Rufus Hoyle — that his troubles really begin . . .

THE MYSTERY OF SILVER FALLS

I. J. Parnham

The whole town turns out to watch the first train journey when the bridge at Silver Falls is completed, but the day turns sour when Kane Cresswell and his gang arrive. They raid the train and, in the ensuing chaos, $50,000 falls into the river, seemingly lost forever. Wyndham Shelford is determined to find the missing money, but when bodies start washing up, unconventional lawman Lloyd Drake arrives. He is convinced the train raid wasn't everything it seemed . . .